Lotus

Lazlo Ferran

Lotus

Lazlo Ferran

PRINTING HISTORY
Second Edition

Printed in 12 point Times New Roman

Published by Future City Publishing, London.

Visit the Lazlo Ferran blog to see what I am currently working on:
http://bit.ly/12nFGgI

Cover:
Graphics: Pixel Studio Banjaluka
Purple lotus flower photo: morguefile.com/creative/pjhudson
Blacklotus abstract: morguefile.com/creative/quicksandala

Acknowledgments

Thanks to Pedro Diaz and L for helping me to bring this project to fruition.

The lotus is seen as the symbol for enlightenment, purity or rebirth in Buddhism and eternity in Hinduism.

Contents

The Steps 11
The Detective 17
The Steps 51
The Castle 53
The Steps 83
Leviathan 87
The Steps 111
Friar 115
The Steps 141
Painter 145
The Steps 177
Monk 185
The Steps 211
Opium 215

The Steps

I was a very brave man. I died in a trench near Verdun. My sticky limbs became the mud, left behind by the victorious and the living. Mud and rust. Funny how reality so quickly becomes fossilised, becomes history. The detritus of war, tank hulks, rotting flesh and spent cartridges soon become mud and rust.

My name is Robert Lath. At least I cling to the sound of it from a long, long time ago. It seems to me that time only exists as a chronology in our memories and even there it's distorted by emotion and intensity. It becomes hard to judge just how long it is since something happened.

It's hard to know for certain who Robert Lath was. I dig among memories for clues, but the more I dig for bones, the more flesh I unearth. All I feel sure of is that I once wrote thrillers. Historical adventures in the style of Sir Walter Scott or Defoe, mine were not top drawer, but they made me an honest living, some kind of life, much better than death.

***

Another dismembered memory comes to me.

I danced a dance with a sylvan faerie in a wooded glade. The sun beat upon the pollen-lit air, so that slanted columns of light dazzled us and sent our lamb-lilly arms out to groan with the gained day. We were immortal, sun-virgins, and our laughter rippled the hot air while we came down to land on rust-tipped ferns still resplendent in our green desire.

I held her arm-muscle. My finger tips seemed to make her roll onto her back, always an unattainable position in the past. But now I had entered the secret room of her soul like a demon. I had power, I had the key, though I knew not whence it came. I assumed the tiger-mantle, a self other than my usual half-formed self, the whole man each male has known throughout eternity.

The unattainable sable of her skin now rested against my skin, so that she said she no longer needed clothes. They came off as easy as a wheat husk in a child's teeth. I drew supernatural breath to pull the last, silken sheath from her rosy hips and she lay naked as a primrose.

She held my own hot member, as if she could steer our wild ship between the rocks of love. And she did. She steered me right into the dock and, for the first time, I knew love of my self. I had to know it, for part of me had entered her, and without a selfish thread to guide it, that part would have been lost.

But my hands, oh, how they caressed her breasts, her thighs, her smooth buttocks and, oh, how I kissed her lips, as if she could not see that I was inside her.

And then, rising, rising, came the light of deliverance, the spurt to the end of the race, the only race I ever won. But isn't it always so? Then we collapsed around each other like the petals of a flower, beaten by the burning sun.

I don't remember who she was or where it was. I only know that remembering this counters the increasing anger I feel inside while on the steps. Isn't that the only thing that sex ever achieves beside birth; an easing, for a while, of anger?

***

My internal voice had been my only world for an eternity. I spoke and I listened, but I could touch nothing. Not aware, at first, that I had a body, 1 told myself tales about mud and childhood. It occurred to me that, since I could think, I might still have a body. Try as I might, I couldn't find it. I couldn't move until one day – I use the term 'day' in its most abstract form – I felt something brush my cheek. I became aware for the first time that I still *had* a cheek, whereupon I could move my nose and then my mouth. With a hop, skip and a jump, metaphorically speaking, I located my shoulder, my hand, and finally moved a finger. I felt again the touch on my cheek of something cool, like a whisper. It had to be a draft from somewhere.

I believed myself to be in a space that I couldn't see. I sat on a staircase, about four feet wide. I felt a vertical wall to my right a vertical drop to my left. The dank, foul smelling draft came that had brushed my cheek came from the abyss. I dared not move. After what seemed many more months, or years, I began to wonder why I had no need for food or water.

"Never mind," I told myself "This must be some strange dream. I will wake in a minute."

Then I heard the voice and a moment later, I saw the face. nA soft throat-clearing preceded a glowing eminence, which moved swiftly in front of my feet and resolved into a human face. The feature of the face seemed to shift and merge but, try as I might, I couldn't form a clear impression of it. The face told me something, offered me a choice, and then vanished. I still can't picture the face. What it offered I eventually recalled, but more of that later.

***

I started to crawl up the steps. I didn't want to go down. The inky blackness had a malevolence about it which smacked of a staircase to Hell. Indeed, if the staircase did go down and down for something approaching forever, as the dank and foul upward draft promised, then where else could it go but Hell? It seemed faithless, and sacrilegious to even contemplate going down. So I crawled up those stone steps, unyielding and yet not cold to the touch, for many days or weeks.

How could I tell for how long I crawled? I seemed not

to need food or water any more. Not once did I feel the desperate struggle of any insect under the palm of my hand or the touch of anything other than stone. I seemed to be completely alone. I dared not stand for fear of falling. I have never been frightened of heights, suffered the seduction of vertigo, but here I imagined myself falling.

It seemed as I had been musing, for the millionth time, how I might have come to be here, when my head hit something solid, a ceiling. I felt it with my hands and concluded that I could climb no further. Nor could I feel any crack or marking in the horizontal surface above me. My thoughts turned in earnest to, 'Where am I?'

I remembered a TV programme once about an ancient well in Cairo, so deep that, decrepit as it had become now – I mean at the time the programme had been made – one could no longer reach the water. Indeed, the presenter, dressed in nonchalant t-shirt and denims, dropped a stone from the lowest position of safety into the abyss and counted to ten before we heard a distant 'plunk.'

"More than a thousand years old, perhaps two thousand," he said, in reverent tones that echoed to distraction.

Could these stairs be the stairs in Cairo? But then again, what is TV? And in what time had that programme been made? For that matter, what is a programme? Is it just something I have imagined? I'm filled with so many memories of times with no 'TV' and no 'programmes,' just as vivid and real, that I have to question which might be reality and which my imagination.

And who is *He*? Sometimes He comes in my dreams, takes me to a library and shows me books of lives that might be mine or might not. Sometimes He offers me The Choice.

He came to me in my sleep again and took me to his grand library. I can never see Him clearly in the Library. If I look at Him, I see a genial gentleman, but if I catch a glimpse of Him from the corner of my eye, I know it is not so. Immense, carved oak cabinets hold a large number of books, bound in leather of various colours and hues. He claims that every volume records one of my lives.

I said I didn't believe Him so he handed me a book. They never carry an author name, but announce their contents in gold leaf. This one had been entitled The Detective.

***

The Detective

The red 1971 Pontiac LeMans Convertible streaked along the highway at full speed. The muscular driver behind the wheel wore a T-shirt jeans and Ray Bans and on the passenger seat sat an elegant blonde, wearing a light blue dress, decorated with a floral pattern. Her hair flicked over the rest on the top of the seat. She appeared to be asleep.

The car scrap yard looks like a still from a crazy, car orgy movie.

I enjoy solving puzzles and I'm fascinated by people, so I paid half the rent on a small office with a two-bit lawyer I knew in 'Nam and set up shop as a private detective. Yeah. I guess that's how I came to be in this asshole of a dump at 3 am in the morning.

I often talk to myself when I'm working, to relieve the boredom. I talk to myself like a bad voice-over in a cheap B-picture. I always wanted to *be* an actor, maybe because I feel I have lived other lives before. Maybe that's also why people fascinate me so much.

The scrap yard cars still sparkle seductively in the neon glow of Schliemann's Diner and the Penny Laundromat. But I'm more interested in the dim doorway between both establishments. At any moment I expected to see a young Turkish boy emerge from it and walk to his bicycle. The fat man should come out straight after. But after fifteen more minutes, cramp sets in and I have to take a leak. I creep to a rotting car chassis and see the familiar dark colour in my piss. Blood.

I feel too young to die by anything other than a bullet. It's ironic that I survive Vietnam, get back to the States and immediately start pissing blood. It started five years ago. I sometimes have pain on both sides, just below my hips, and I know I am dying. Kidney cancer.

I get back to my vantage point just in time to see the fat man come out. He stops, wipes his brow with a white handkerchief and opens the driver door to a naked Cadillac Eldorado. I memorise the number plate and leave.

***

This case started, as I'd always dreamed one would, with a blonde walking into my office. Actually, she looked better than the blondes I have dreamed of. She had the face of a top call girl, but eyes of an innocent. She looked like my first, my last love and I had been hooked.

I had to take another drag on my cigarette before I could speak:

"Yes? Can I help you?"

"I hope so. I need you to find a killer."

"Whose?"

"My sister's."

I stubbed my cigarette butt out and blew a long stream of white smoke toward the window. "Okay, so why aren't the LAPD interested?"

"They gave up Mister Andrews."

"Right. You have funds?"

"I have what it takes."

"Yeah. Let's just start with the basics." I took out a greasy pro-forma and filled it in while she supplied the answers. When I finished she had lit an expensive cigarette. It floated between her fingers, as if she were trying to stop it drifting away. I told her my rates and asked if she could pay.

"Yes. Okay."

"Sign."

She wore a blue three piece with a very short, tight skirt and a matching hat. Whoever's woman she might be had to be paying for this investigation. I put her at twenty-two.

"I've no doubt … Miss Stevens …" I began, reading her name from the form. "I can find out a good deal from the Court Records, but suppose you tell me what I won't find there?"

"Alright. My sister, older sister by two years, was murdered, shot near the corner of Sunset and Vine, late one night, while leaving a restaurant and walking to a car. The car belonged to Johnny Chico. Here's her photo." She pulled a folded, glossy 10x8 from her handbag, opened it up and lay it in front of me.

"She looks just like you. Could be your twin?" The blonde opposite nodded noncommittally.

"I'm going with him now. He likes young blondes." She blew a plume of white smoke to emphasise her point. "I have reason to believe it's Johnny's ex who had my sister shot. Susan would not have done anything to deserve being shot. I believe it was to punish Johnny. I want you to find the killer."

"I presume Johnny is paying for this."

"Yes, but he tried to stop me. You see, I think his ex, Stella, wants to kill *me* now. She is only interested in money. If I don't catch the killer, and her, it will be my head on her plate next."

"I don't understand. He tried to stop you?"

"Yes. Said it was too dangerous."

"But he's paying for this?"

"It's only a loan. He said if I wanted to go through with it, he would help me out."

"I see." She stubbed her cigarette out in my dirty ashtray. I could see bright pink lipstick on the butt. My groin reacted. I had to concentrate. Beauty in this city is dangerous, probably is everywhere. "There's a lot to think about here, but tell me, why me? If you have access to money, I'm not the best you can afford."

"Oh but you are. I heard from a colleague that you are dying. Is that true?"

"Miss Stevens… I don't think that…"

"Well, I also heard that there is a new experimental treatment for your cancer. Radiotherapy? That will take money. This case will be risky. I need a man who can take more risks than usual."

I smiled.

"Okay Miss Stevens, I w-…" Without completing my sentence, I leaped out of my seat and caught the girl's head, just before it hit the floor.

She murmured incoherently. I picked her up and set her back in the chair. My colleague's face appeared in his doorway.

"What's up?" he said.

"It's alright Jack. Have you still got that whiskey?"

"Yeah! I'll bring it." He fussed over her when he brought the glass of spirit.

"Okay. She'll be fine Jack. It's alright. Leave me alone with her." He closed the door reluctantly.

The girl drained the glass.

"Where am I?" she murmured. "Why am I wearing these clothes?"

"You're in my office and you're quite safe. I think you just fainted. Jason Andrews, your Private Investigator."

I felt like a fraud.

"A PI? That's funny!"

"Why?"

"I was going to hire one!"

"You just did! Me!"

"Really? Then you can help me?"

"I'll do my best. Are you sure you have told me everything Johnny knows?"

"Who's Johnny? And why am I wearing these clothes?"

"Okay. I think I'd better call for a doctor or ambulance."

"No! No, I'd rather you didn't. I'll be fine after a little rest. I just need to know who Johnny is and why I'm in these clothes."

"You hired me to find the killer of your sister, Susan. You're wearing those clothes because Johnny Chico paid for them."

"Oh no, not Chico. That can't be right! Mister Andrews, I have something to tell you in confidence. I have been diagnosed, by a rather expensive private doctor, with schizophrenia. Twice since my diagnosis I have come home in the early hours drunk and with bad bruising. *Many times* I have come back drunk and some nights I don't come back at all. That's what my mother told me. *I* have no memory of these things. It was her who arranged for the doctor. Now I have the treatment, I want the facts. Where do I go on these nights? That's what I came here to hire you for."

I couldn't believe what I had just heard! Two cases from the same person and the solution to one case right in front of my eyes. I began to wonder if somebody was pulling my leg or if it was Christmas.

"Don't tell anyone about my condition. And if you find the killer, will you let me know?"

"Ha! Sure."

***

Johnny Chico! Small-time drug-hustler. I haven't heard from him in years! So he's moved up in the world. Should be no problem to track him down now. And then… easy money!

It all looked so *easy*. I staked out Miss Stevens' house the following morning and recorded that she left shortly after 7 pm, wearing jeans and a baggy t-shirt. She took a bus to China Town, walked a few blocks and then entered a doorway next to a grocer. She re-emerged mid-evening on the arm of Johnny Chico. While she looked a million dollars, he looked rich, but mostly a lot older. He walked her to a red '71 Pontiac LeMans Convertible, so I took the license plate. I had earned my first fifty bucks and now I needed to do a bit more digging about Elizabeth, Susan and Chico.

For ten bucks and a coffee my favourite grass, Digger, told me he would find out what he could about Chico. I staked out Elizabeth's house again on a whim and discovered that she always came home wearing casual clothes and always in the early hours. On the third morning I saw an older woman leaving the house. I took a risk.

"Missus Stevens!" I shouted, jumping out of the car. "Can I speak to you for a moment? I'm an LAPD detective investigating the death of your daughter, Susan."

"I have nothing more to say! You can turn around and go home young man!" She had a slight accent, perhaps Greek.

"Just one question… it's important for the safety of Elizabeth…"

"She's in danger too? Oh my God! Make it quick. If the neighbours see us…"

"I just want to ask if anybody besides you, Elizabeth, myself and the doctor responsible, know about her schizophrenia. She has only told me in the strictest confidentiality."

"What is this? *Nobody* should know about *that*!"

"Missus *Stevens*!" She turned and walked away.

At least I knew that Elizabeth told the truth and that her mother *knew* about the schizophrenia. I knew something else; Mrs Stevens was scared.

I visited a private clinic, put down a deposit of $500 on a course of the radiotherapy and went looking for Digger.

"Chico's boss is Sadek," he told me. "But there's something else. Something big's going down."

"Okay." I thumbed off a $5 note.

"In the next week, I think. Sadek is expecting a big delivery and a large part of it is going to Chico. An *unusually* large part."

Josef Sadek was one of the most feared crime bosses in LA. If the Sicilian Mafia were terrifying, the Turks were worse. Nobody understood a mind-set that would boil a man's cock, have it stitched inside his lover's vagina, her breasts stitched to his chest and both thrown together into the river, just to please his wife. It looked quite possible that one of Sadek's men had killed Susan, perhaps to punish Chico. Sadek allegedly used many hit-men, the most feared only known by the nickname, Blue. I decided I had to establish for myself a direct link between Sadek and Chico. This wouldn't be hard to do. Sadek had a runner, a young Turkish boy called Farrouk, who often spoke to police informants. This had proved convenient for all; Sadek fed us false information, occasionally good information on rivals, and we fed him the same.

That's how I came to be on the stake-out in the scrap yard.

***

Sadek was the fat man. When I left the scene I thought a blue Ford van followed me for a few blocks, but I couldn't be sure.

Farrouk's home was common knowledge, so I hung around outside his tenement the following morning. He collected Marvel comics, so I picked up a rare one for five bucks before I went and held it out when he passed on his bicycle.

"Hey Mister!" he said, stepping of his sliding bike. "What issue is that?" I held up the front cover. "Nice! Can I buy it off you?"

"No need. You can have it. Just a small piece of information…"

"Like what?"

"Like; do you know if Sadek works directly with Johnny Chico?"

"Um. I have seen them both eating together a few times in Dino's. That's about it."

"When was this?"

"Hey! My mother can't bury a comic!" He grabbed the comic, stuffed it in his jacket, strode to the bike and rode off.

Now I had a connection.

***

I have started to have bad dreams too. I kept seeing this red Pontiac going over a cliff. It could be Chico's, but it feels like a nightmare! I needed a break. On Saturday morning I shut up shop and took my old grey Chevy out of the City, heading north east. I drove past my parent's old farm and on to Death Valley National Park where I used to spend the fall break with my dad as a kid. I sat on lip of a bluff, ate a cold burger drizzled with sauce, drank a lukewarm beer and watched an old buzzard for hours. Just as the sun began to set, my mind came down from the sky and I began to think:

How much longer have I got? I don't really want to wait for renal failure, or worse… So probably a big risk is worth it; chances are if I die, I only die a bit earlier and at least it's quick. Okay, I am gonna do this.

So what did I have? Sadek was getting something big. It had to be heroin. It's what he was famous for. I really didn't see Sadek killing Chico's girl for punishment, unless he did it in the open, to set an example. Chico wasn't close enough for him to get too personal. And yet the killer hadn't been caught. But it could have been one of Sadek's hit men, if Chico wanted it… if Sadek wanted to do him a favour or Chico had the money. That would be a big debt, the kind that could cement a good working relationship, for a while. Maybe this big delivery was Chico's chance to pay off the debt.

I could try to find out if it was one of Sadek's best men by digging around at LAPD, find out why they dropped it.

And why the hell was Johnny Chico paying for me to track down the killer? Did he want to pin something on

Sadek, a kind of takeover attempt, or is he setting Elizabeth up? Or both?

Hm, could be…

I drove back to the City, checked into the office and put in a call to Tulare, but got no answer.

***

"Miss Stevens called," Jack told me. "I just happened to be passing through."

I called her at 8.01 pm and she picked up the receiver in less than two rings.

"Mister Roberts?"

"Call me Jason."

"Oh! I'm so glad you called. I'm so scared! Can we meet tonight?"

"Sure. Where?"

"Rodeo Burgers on St. Andrews. You know it?"

"Sure."

At 9.05 pm she walked in, wearing jeans, a blouse and a primrose, knitted cardigan.

Off the scale!

"What… can I do for you?" I asked.

"I think somebody followed me. Sorry! Had to go around a block and through an arcade. I think I lost him."

"I think it's my fault. I think Chico knows about your schizophrenia. You've probably been followed for a while, but now he wants us *both* to know we're being watched."

"You're being watched too?"

"Yes, but not by Chico's men, by Sadek's. And for a different reason"

"Who's Sadek?"

"Some big card, crime boss round here."

"You think he killed Susan?"

"No, he's too big to do dirty work! Listen, do you know what triggers your state-of-mind switches, I mean when you become the *other* Elizabeth? I'm betting Chico doesn't have you followed *then*. We could maybe use it to trick them…"

"No. Sorry. I think it's me, and some part of me seems to plan it. I go out, meaning to meet somebody or go somewhere, but then I come back late in the morning tired. But that's what I wanted to talk to you about… I mean apart from being followed…"

Her words came out in a breathless tumble, so I ordered her a milkshake – her choice – a coffee for me and two burgers. I hadn't been able to eat since hearing her message.

"Go on," I prompted, with a mouth full of burger.

"Oh. The point is that I don't feel safe at home now. My mother doesn't understand all this… she's just a first generation Greek immigrant. My younger sister, Tereza, is too young to understand. My father is long dead. I have no-one … except *you*! I find that I only feel safe with *you*! I know it sounds silly…"

"No! Not at all. Listen, there is something you don't know about me. I am dying. Of cancer."

"Oh no!" She reached out and placed her hand on mine. I pulled it away reflexively, so she placed her hand flat on the table.

"My father's gone," I continued, "and my older brother doesn't want to know me. My mother died a long time ago. We have a lot in common."

"I have an idea!"

"What? Pass the tomato sauce, please."

"What if you … um guard me tonight? That Chico guy can't possibly miss me for one night. I *often* stay at home. Then I will feel much safer."

"How do you *know* he won't miss you? Perhaps you… and he, planned something tonight."

"Ha! Ha! Yes, I hadn't thought of *that*."

"No. I don't think it's a good idea. We're being watched. If we spend too much time together, he'll get jealous. And from what I hear, when Chico gets jealous, things happen, bad things."

I put the last mouthful of burger in my mouth, wiped my hands on the paper napkin and placed my hands on the table, ready to get up.

"How about this?" she murmured, reaching out again and touched my finger tips with hers. Her eyes welled with tears. "Please?" she asked. I took her hand and squeezed it.

Fool!

"There's this little motel I know, north of the city. I used to go there as a teenager with girls … ."

"Really? How exciting! Does that mean you're going to seduce me?"

"Ha!"

We reached the motel, a desolate place with a blue neon sign wafted by the slight breeze on a hot night. The crickets set up a symphony of 'creeks' while we flopped on the cheap, double bed.

As the car headlights played across the ceiling my fingers travelled across her cheek.

"Elizabeth," I murmured.

"Call me Liz or Lizzie. You know… Jason, *I*, at least, am still a virgin. I have no experience of men, although I know my alter-ego does. I wondered for a long time why I was no longer physically a virgin and sometimes woke up with unexplained bruising around my hips. Mr Chico is probably *not* a gentleman! How do you feel about a woman as inexperienced as me?" She stared up at the ceiling.

I moved my fingers to her chin and then lightly rested them on the mound of her breast. "Sex is not a skill, it's something you explore together with somebody you love. It doesn't matter that you're a virgin. All women *are* with a new man."

She grasped my wrist and turned to face me. I stared into those blue eyes and melted. My cock strained to get out of my Levis, but I only became momentarily aware of it.

"Lizzie, you are *so* beautiful."

"Oh *yeah*? My mother says I have a big nose and buck-teeth! The boys at school didn't seem to think much different! They never even groped me!"

"You probably don't have a sensitive enough bum to have detected them!"

"Ha! Ha!" She suddenly leaned into me and put her lips to mine. We kissed furiously. Each of her kisses seemed to demand that we be naked. I slid my hand inside her bra, but she had already begun unbuttoning her blouse. I unclasped her bra and pulled off my own t-shirt, before unzipping my jeans. I had only just yanked them and my briefs over my hips when she presented her breasts to my mouth. She hauled her bra up, like a halter, around her neck. This excited me. She seemed frantic to have me inside her and shoved her jeans and panties down to her ankles, before kicking them off.

I felt breathless at the speed and excessiveness of her nakedness.

She climbed onto me, I entered her but when she pummelled me like a fighting child, I almost stopped.

"No! Don't stop!"

***

In the early hours I woke and fetched a cold beer and coke from reception. Lizzie still had her bra wrapped around her neck when I left her, but when I opened the door, I saw her kneeling on the bed with her legs open. Her hands were bound behind her back by her bra. For a moment I the scene seemed confused, so I looked around the room for another man.

"Don't worry," She murmured. "Johnny taught me how to do a lot of things with underwear."

"Elizabeth?"

"Lizbet. You can call me Lizbet. And what are *you* doing here anyhow Mister Roberts. Oh it doesn't matter… I guess you're just another one of Johnny's business partners. He regularly asks me to do this sort of thing for him. I'm only too happy to oblige, but you lay one finger on me… I mean, you hurt me and you'll be dead before noon. Only Johnny Chico does *that* to me! Where do you want me?"

"I … ."

"On the floor? Why don't you just fuck me on the floor? Do anything you like to me, as long as you don't hurt or scar me. I'm pretty tough you know."

I fucked her, harder and harder and then shouted, "Yes!"

"I'm tired," she told me when we finished. "Don't try and fuck me in my sleep. I don't like it. Wake me first." She reached around and kissed me. Her kiss tasted like a blow-back.

The next thing I know I'm waking up and the sunlight, through the dusty window is highlighting the contours of her back.

"Lizbet, we need to move. Are you awake?"

"Um. Lizbet? Why did you call me that?" She rolled over and I stared into those blue oceans.

"Sorry Elizabeth. It was a mistake…"

"No it wasn't. Unless you knew my birth name was Lizbet?" I didn't know what to say. "She was here, wasn't she? My alter-ego? Is that what she likes to be called?" Then she noticed the bra on one of her wrists. "Did you tie me *up*?" she asked.

"*No*! She did it herself? I mean *you* did!"

"Hm! What did you say about going?" She had already started getting dressed, but it took her a while to find her panties. I brought the car round and while I drove back toward the City, she stayed silent, avoiding my gaze. I didn't much mind.

"Thank you God!" I said silently. "It doesn't get you off the hook for letting me die so young… But thank you anyway!"

I loved them both but Lizzie was my little Corvette.

***

I dropped her at a bus stop and told her to be careful. After showering and changing my clothes, I was on my way back to the office. I remembered having a dream about the Pontiac again:

The red 1971 Pontiac LeMans Convertible streaked along the highway at full speed. The muscular driver behind the wheel wore a T-shirt jeans and Ray Bans. The air-stream over the windscreen ruffled his medium-length brown hair violently. He held the accelerator flat to the floor with his foot and seemed only intent only on the road ahead. The speedo needle hovered just above the 130 mph mark. On the passenger seat sat an elegant blonde, wearing a light blue dress, decorated with a floral pattern. Her hair flicked over the rest on the top of the seat. She appeared to be asleep. A small patch of red blood slowly spread out on her stomach. The car raced on.

I guessed I would see the blue van, but I had been wrong.

It was only 6.23 am and the road was almost deserted. I wasn't even two blocks from my apartment when a black '65 Ford Galaxy pulled up alongside at some lights, a Colt 45 protruding from the passenger-side window.

"Leave the car running Mister Andrews and get in the back. Mister Sadek wants to talk to you."

Twenty, short minutes later they strapped me into a big black chair.

"Having a loaded .45 inside your mouth for any length of time is inconvenient Mister Roberts, I know that, but I have become curious about you. I *know* you are curious about me."

I won't bore you with the details of what happened

next. Let's just say that I know, very well, what a large amount of electricity passing through your balls feels like. Eventually, I had to tell Sadek what I knewm, but I convinced him Elizabeth's schizophrenia was a lie.

I spent at least two days in the 'pens,' in a large cellar. Most of the time I dreamed.

Two visions, however, I had seen before, many times during my life. In one I seem to be a medieval knight, living with a beautiful woman called Éloïse. In the other I live on board a gigantic spaceship, carrying freight from Mars. But this time they seemed far too real for dreams.

Some of my dreams were of lying in a luxury hotel, but when I regained enough consciousness to see that my bed was a flea-ridden mattress, I laughed. It didn't seem so funny when I understood that I had become addicted to heroin.

Sadek had me released downtown, just before dawn. One of his heavies handed me a small packet of high-grade H as a leaving present.

I had no money, so I made my way to the office where I told Jack the trouble I was in.

***

I found a letter at my apartment; my car had been impounded.

Great!

Anger burned inside me. I hadn't envisaged chasing the dragon during my last few months. The fire inside me burned for Sadek and there would be only way I could extinguish the flames; revenge! I didn't like to think of myself as a vengeful man, but with possibly less than a year to live, revenge suddenly looked like an attractive option. Sadek *had* to be afraid of me. What he had done made little sense otherwise. Was he afraid because he really had arranged Susan's death, perhaps carried out the hit himself? I would find out and make him suffer in a way he had never imagined.

I paid for my car's release with a cheque. I took out the last cash I had, $700 in $50s, at the bank and left for Elizabeth's, already feeling the need for another heroin hit. On the way I stopped off to talk to Digger. In return for a $100 bill and a warning to get out of town for a while, he told me that Sadek could possibly once have been a hit-man, fought in World War Two, was a good dancer under the name of Three Feet and had a wife and invalid daughter living at Beverly Hills; 820 North Cannon Drive.

"Okay. Another thing… Who do you see around here if you want to hire a hit man?" I asked

"Well, Woody's your best bet, if you got a grand; bar-fly down on Sunset. If you want the best, there's Blue…"

"Yeah. I know."

"One last thing… Did you learn anything more about that… delivery?"

"Five days. Don't know time or place, but most likely on the outskirts of town. Sadek's not the top man in the chain and he'll have to make a big payment. It will be somewhere isolated, somewhere he can have privacy, perhaps somewhere he employs a lot of men. I know the *Municipal Dump* men are in his pocket."

***

"Get in the car!" I shouted, when Lizzie opened the door. "We're not safe *anywhere*!"

"Where have you been?"

"Staying as a guest of Sadek."

"Oh my God! Did he hurt you? You look terrible."

"Yes."

While we drove round town I outlined my plan. I wanted her to pose as 'Lizbet' and borrow $100,000 from Chico, to hire Blue. My idea to draw Blue out by acting as bait myself didn't draw too much enthusiasm from her. But I explained that Sadek and Chico seemed scared of me because the knew that I knew that Chico had paid for

Susan's murder. She became enthusiastic when I told her that Chico would probably be ordering a hit on her too, any day. If Sadek was Blue, I would capture him and ransom him for a million dollars. I gave her my cousin's number in New York and told her to leave a message there when she had set up a hit with Woody on Sunset, details of precisely at which bar to follow later.

"This is crazy!" she told me.

"Well, I haven't worked out all the details yet. Listen, there are two things I haven't told you."

"Okay," she said, taking a deep breath. "You're never short of surprises."

"Sadek has got me hooked on heroin. I need to pick up some in the next hour, or *you're* gonna have to drive *me* around."

"And the other?"

"This is risky. I know that. But I need to take risks. I have a daughter."

"Oh… Oh?"

"I was married before Nam. When I came back it was all over. But I have a daughter, Chloe, in Tulare. She's five now. Her mum is in and out of work… she's an alcoholic. I don't want Chloe to be without the money for a really good start in life."

***

I felt like a bum when I found a quiet parking lot and shot up. I must have fallen asleep, because I checked the time and half an hour had passed since I parked. I turned the ignition key and made for the main library, to dig up whatever I could find on Sadek's past.

The library's tall tower nearly put me off, because I have an ineplicable phobia for long flights of steps. Fortunately, I could find what I wanted closer to the ground, but I didn't find much. Just before closing time I found a photograph, dated February, 1942, of the polka winner in a dancing competition, named as 'Three Feet'

Sadek. He looked like the Josef Sadek I knew, but something wasn't quite right.

Perhaps it's because he was a lot younger. His face looks too thin. Why's he not using his full name? Maybe a draft-dodger.

I discovered that conscription had started in 1940, so draft-dodging seemed a plausible explanation, but I would have to return the following day to find out more.

Nobody answered on the Tulare number. I spent the night curled around a bottle of Jack Daniels in a quiet lay-by, out of town.

***

The red 1971 Pontiac LeMans Convertible streaked along the highway at full speed. The muscular driver behind the wheel wore a T-shirt jeans and Ray Bans. The air-stream over the windscreen ruffled his medium-length brown hair violently. He held the accelerator flat to the floor with his foot and seemed only intent only on the road ahead. The speedo needle hovered just above the 130 mph mark. On the passenger seat sat an elegant blonde, wearing a light blue dress, decorated with a floral pattern. Her hair flicked over the rest on the top of the seat. She appeared to be asleep. A small patch of red blood slowly spread out on her stomach. The car raced on.

A mile ahead the road veered to the right, just short of a cliff, overlooking a deep canyon. Danger signs had lined the road for the last quarter mile and a wooden fence stood on the side of the road nearest the edge. Some distance behind the speeding Pontiac came a green Mustang and a naked Cadillac.

In the morning, I left a message containing Woody's location at my cousin's, returned to the library and continued to dig. At last I found what I had been looking for in an edition of the Los Angeles Times, dated 1938:

Ablak Sadek, winner of the third prize for the
Foxtrot, is very happy with the reward money
of $20.

Ablak and his two sons stared out of a grainy
photograph. I could instantly see the facial resemblance
of the father to Josef and his sons. The only question had
to be; which one is Josef? I looked at the war-time
obituary for the period of the Korean War and found what
I sought:

Altay Sadek, aged 19, missing in action.

An accompanying photograph showed a young man
who looked like Josef Sadek, so I compared the
photograph with that of the dance competition winner.
They looked similar, but not the same. I left feeling
satisfied:

"Josef Sadek *must be* 'Three Feet.'"

When I called my cousin to check if there were any
messages, he told me that Elizabeth had met a hit man,
but not Blue. I called an hour later and heard a garbled
message about a location across town. I jumped in cab
and, after nearly two hours of driving to different
locations, finding a phone box to call my cousin from and
then driving to a new location, I had run out of money.

"Okay. Wait up by the phone! If I don't call by 2 am,
call the LAPD." I told the cabbie, when we reached an
alleyway, off North Broadway.

"You gotta be joking man! I ain't waiting here! I got
what *I* need and I'm outta here! Good luck!"

*I'm completely unprepared for this! I don't even have a
torch! Just the .22, which is probably be useless anyway
against this joker!*

Edging round the corner into the alleyway, I could see
nothing suspicious. After about fifty yards, the alleyway

opened up into some kind of back lot. There were a few wrecked cars and piles of smashed packing crates and in a corner lay an old mattress, upon which some winos sat, talking in low voices.

"Did you see a girl go this way?" I asked.

They looked suspicious, so I held out my last dollar bill. Instantly, they all pointed to another alleyway that led off the back lot. I edged toward it and once inside, I could see it would make a good killing zone.

All the lights had been knocked out and I could see two sets of fire-escape steps, the left one pulled down. I heard something and stopped in my tracks. I listened and heard again something that reminded me of the low crying from my heroin-soaked dreams in the pens.

It could be a trap!

I could hear only a deathly silence in the alleyway now but I could almost taste the presence of death. I could certainly taste my own fear. I waited, with a bead of sweat running down my temple, until I heard slow steps on the fire escape. They were coming closer, climbing and still I waited until something blue flickered in the pale light penetrating the alley from a distant street lamp.

Surely this is not him? Could it be? Should I shoot now? Has he killed Lizzie?

My mind became a tumult of conflicting emotions and strategies. My gun remained fixed at my shin by indecision. Then the footsteps, sounding curiously like high heeled ones, reached the alley way itself and still I waited.

Into view came Lizzie, weeping.

"Lizzie!" I whispered. I reached for her and she tumbled into my arms.

"Jason! Oh thank God! I was so scared."

"Are you alright?"

"I think so. He took the money. He was on the fire escape above me. He had a gun pointing at me. I could see it."

"Okay, let's get out of here."

I took her back to North Broadway and hailed a cab back to my car. Her breath came in little, shuddering gasps. Only when I started driving, did she began to calm down.

"He was so creepy! So fat!"

"Really? Tell me everything you can remember."

"Okay. I'll try. He had a black balaclava on, so I couldn't see his face. He wore only black clothes. There was really nothing else distinctive I could say, except his voice."

"What about it?"

"Very high pitched. Like a woman. Oh, he really scared me."

"What did he say?"

"Just said, 'Leave the money there. I am pointing a gun at your head. I know what to do. It will be done within four days. If you try to follow me or interfere in any way, you will die, for free. You understand?' I nodded and he was gone!"

***

I left the office the following noon and scouted around. Since I normally ate in for lunch, I guessed Blue would not be watching me yet. I found what I wanted only three blocks from the office. A narrow alley, not dissimilar to the one where Lizzie had made the drop for Blue, had a fire-escape on only one side and steps, half way along it, down to a basement. It had one or two aspects that were to my advantage, however. I then called a friend, an ex-ballistics officer, who ran a gun-shop, told him what I wanted and that I would come over at noon the following day to pick it up.

"Phew! That's a little bit special," he replied. "Might take me time to dig out that kinda stuff. What caliber? What you going after?"

"Never mind the caliber. Anything will do."

I bought a roll of duct-tape, two identical black t-shirts and a distinctive bright blue cap from Wal-Mart and put them in my car, which I moved to a car park on the other side of the alleyway I had found. I left and attempted to do a normal afternoon's work.

***

At 6 pm I went home and made a burger, before taking a nap for an hour. Then I drove back into town, wearing the black t-shirt, parked the car in the same place and walked through the alleyway I had found to a gym I knew, near the office. Blue wouldn't kill me this time, but it still made me shake with nerves. I hadn't worked out for years, so after thirty minutes I felt exhausted. I had a coffee and read some magazines in the café, passing the time until 10.30. In September there would still light until 9.15 in Los Angeles. I wanted it to be dark, so that Sadek would make his kill.

The following noon the gun shop owner took me to a locked room, pulled a sheet off a table and pointed to the items laid out, with his eye brows raised.

"Five rounds of tranquilizers, $24 a pop, one .50 tranquilizer gun at $400 and one AN/PVS-2 Starlight infra-red sight at $200. You sure about this?"

"Sure. Here you go," I replied, handing him the fold of notes. "Pack it all for me in something anonymous." I handed him another ten bucks.

At 7.40 pm I walked to the car, still wearing the black t-shirt and blue cap, and noted the blue van parked across the road. I took the duffle bag from the trunk, placed it on the passenger seat and drove slowly out of town. As I expected the van followed me and I pulled over to assemble the rifle and put it in the bag. The van had parked behind me, so I continued driving north until I came to a quiet junction. Turning the car into a lane behind some trees, I quickly took up position with the gun and hoped the tranquilizers weren't meant for elephants.

It didn't take me long to knock out the driver, ambush the inevitable man in the back and drive the van to a quiet location. I bound the driver's mouth and hands with duct-tape and dragged the other man to my car. I considered killing him, but instead took out my syringe and injected him with a nice dose of junk, knowing I could always get more in town. I left the syringe and empty packet next to him and returned to the van with my own car keys, the rifle and the other paraphernalia.

Should take him time to get anywhere tied up with that in his veins and no keys!

I dragged the driver into the back of the van and headed for town. Arriving at the gym's parking lot at 9.45 pm, I climbed into the back of the van.

"You and I are gonna have a little talk!" I him. He looked terrified. I guessed him to be no real hard man himself, little more than a driver. This suited my purposes nicely. I ripped off his t-shirt and took out a switch-blade. "All you have to do is nod for 'yes' and shake your head for 'no.'"

He nodded vigorously.

I worked him over pretty well with my knife for forty minutes, before telling him:

"I know a quiet place near here. I'm gonna drive you there and let you out."

I drove the van and parked it with the front pointing directly at the west end of the alley.

"Okay. See this?" I said, pulling out the rifle. He nodded quickly. "You've seen what I can do with it. I'm gonna stay here with the van until you get through that alley to the main street beyond. You can get a cab there. Any funny stuff and I'm gonna fire. Only this time it's elephant tranquilizer."

He nodded.

"Okay. Here! Take this t-shirt, I always keep a spare, and this cap. You look a mess." I ripped off his gag.

"Hey, thanks man!"

I slapped the cap on his head and threw him the t-shirt. He pulled on the t-shirt, put the cap on and climbed out of the van by the back door at 10.30 pm.

"No *noise* now! I'm watching!" I said.

I had no more than a moment to watch him before I had to move. I jumped out the back of the van with the rifle and climbed the ladder onto the roof. I had begun to think he would make it all the way, that Blue wasn't there that night, when he suddenly dropped to the ground.

It's you or me now Blue. Killing one of your own! Shame! But now I have the proof... Josef Sadek!

My breathing slowed almost to a stop while I focused through the infra-red sight. I held my index finger delicately over the trigger and waited. Minutes went by without me seeing any movement.

Surely he has to move!

I saw the faintest variation in light on the second floor landing of the fire-escape.

Is it a cat? A branch of some flower in a pot, moving in a breeze? But there is no breeze!

I re-aligned the barrel to the point of movement. Then I saw another, on the steps below the first point.

Something is coming down.

I still had no view of the target, just a patch of darkness, like the background.

For a fat man he sure is stealthy. But then again; Korea. I have to be very, very careful.

The killer stooped over the body on the ground. I had no doubt that it was Sadek. I still couldn't see his head, but I didn't need to. I lined up on his shoulder and gently, oh so gently, squeezed the trigger. The large body slumped over the one beneath. I could hardly believe my luck as I clambered down and stealthily walked to the two bodies. I kicked Sadek's body, but he didn't react.

Have to move fast!

Running back to the van, I slung the rifle in the back and pulled a camera out of my bag. Taking a quick snap from a distance I ran over to the two bodies and took photographs, from four angles, of them, making sure to show Sadek's sniper rifle, which lay by his side. He wore a black balaclava, so I pulled it off to take another photograph, but stopped.

It's not Sadek! I would know his face anywhere! Who the fuck is this?

The face looked uncannily like Sadek's, but fatter. I had an uncomfortable idea who it might be. However, this didn't change my basic plan. I took the black cotton gloves off the fat man, put his fingerprints on his rifle, dragged his heavy body to the van, piled it into the back and drove to an isolated lane, outside the City.

"Who the *fuck* are you?" I asked the fat man. I had sat him up on the van's bench and I ripped the duct tape from his mouth.

"Kill me!" he yelled, with an unexpected alto timbre. When he began to sob in a high pitch timbre I immediately remembered the high-pitched crying in Sadek's basement. This had to be the same man. When Lizzie told me that Blue spoke in a high voice, I had assumed Sadek had been covering up his real voice, but now I knew this wasn't true. What a fool I'd been.

"I can't kill you! I need money. If you're not Josef Sadek, then… who are you?"

"I'm Three Feet. You should see me dance!"

"What?"

The moon face suddenly brightened and I found myself staring into two, innocent, green eyes.

This guy's totally nuts!

"But *Josef* is Three Feet!"

The moon face slowly shook from side to side, as if not sure of himself. "No… I'm Three Feet. Joey's not as good at dancing."

"Joey? Josef?"

Suddenly the moon face looked hurt. His lips clamped shut.

"You're Altay, aren't you?"

"I haven't *got* any money!" he replied angrily. "Look at my arm, my feet, my dong!" He suddenly sounded lucid.

"What?" I ripped his shirt from his fat shoulder and pull it down his arm. Everywhere I looked his arm was black and scarred with needle marks. "You're an addict! Shit! So that's it! Sadek has been hiding you. But how did you survive Korea?"

"Played the game." Altay looked into the far distance and a vacant look came into his eyes. "Yes, that was it. Played the game. Played it until they *all* died. And then Joey came for me. He *saved* me!"

I slumped against the back of the driver seat, beaten. What could I do now? Blue, Altay or Three Feet, as he liked to call himself, was now the only card I had to use in a deadly round of poker with Sadek. But Sadek probably held the better hand. I drove Altay to the motel, tied him to the bed and called Lizzie. No response.

Deciding to use an old-fashioned method to send my demands to Sadek, I wrapped a note wrapped round a brick and lobbed it through his office window.

Call this before 5 am or Altay dies.

I added the number of a phone booth on the edge of town. The call came at 4.59 pm when I made my demands in more detail:

"One million made out to my account and paid in… before the exchange." I heard only silence on the other end of the telephone for nearly a minute, when a familiar voice said:

"Alright. Anything else?"

"Yes. Come alone to the exchange. Where?"

After I ended the call I propped up the sleeping monster on the bed and took a few portrait photographs. Carefully taping a label with his full name onto the camera, I stuck it into his big paws, to cover it in fingerprints, left the camera on the bed and manhandled the monster into another Chevy, which I had hotwired.

Dance out of that, Three Feet!

***

The red 1971 Pontiac LeMans Convertible streaked along the highway at full speed. The muscular driver behind the wheel wore a T-shirt jeans and Ray Bans. The air-stream over the windscreen ruffled his medium-length brown hair violently. He held the accelerator flat to the floor with his foot and seemed only intent only on the road ahead. The speedo needle hovered just above the 130 mph mark. On the passenger seat sat an elegant blonde, wearing a light blue dress, decorated with a floral pattern. Her hair flicked over the rest on the top of the seat. She appeared to be asleep. A small patch of red blood slowly spread out on her stomach. The car raced on.

A mile ahead the road veered to the right, just short of a cliff overlooking a deep canyon. Danger signs had lined the road for the last quarter mile and a wooden fence stood on the side of the road nearest the edge. Some distance behind the speeding Pontiac came a green Mustang and a naked Cadillac.

Seeing the warning signs the driver grinned and put his head back. He felt the wind roaring around his ears, slapping his face with his hair, and then the Pontiac crashed through the fence.

***

I arrived at the Municipal Dumping Ground north of the city, just in time for the exchange, after picked up a dose of H for both Three Feet and I on the way. We had both stopped shaking and the H had also stopped the pain in my kidneys, something for which I tried to feel grateful. Three Feet lay asleep in the back of the Chevy while I tried the Tulare number one last time, desperate to talk to Chloe.

"Daddy?" she replied when she heard my voice. "Where are you? When are you coming to visit?"

It nearly broke my heart to tell her:

"I can't baby. Not now."

"I couldn't sleep last night daddy. My tummy hurt. Even Freddie didn't help!"

My heart felt like it would burst at the mention of the teddybear I had bought for her last Christmas. I knew she slept with it every night.

"If I had been there, I would have told you a story."

"Tell me one now!"

"But it's midday!"

"So?"

"Okay. Let me think. Um. There was once a teddy who had a button on his tummy and the little girl who owned him had been told not to press the button until she had grown up."

"Really? Like a belly button?"

"No. A red button. Anyway, do you know what she did?"

"No."

"She loved her daddy so much that she didn't press the button at all!"

"Never?"

"Not until she was eighteen. She was a very good girl. And do you know what happened then?"

"No…"

"The teddybear changed into a handsome prince and married her!"

"Oh daddy! I miss you so much. When can I see you?"

"Next week darling. I will come to see you. Okay?"

"Okay…"

"I have to go. Bye bye. I love you loads."

She probably answered, but I had to put the receiver down, so that I could get moving.

I suddenly wondered if my meagre life insurance policy would pay out on cancer; I hadn't had the time to check. Then I briefly wondered if it paid out on death by gun-fight.

At the gate to the Municipal Dump there were two black Ford Thunderbirds, sitting like sentinels on either side of the metal barrier. Inside, the road had well-cut grass either side on banks leading up to loosely planted trees, giving the impression of the approach to a sanatorium or crematorium. I looked at the angle of the bank and the gates in my mirrors.

Then I saw the parked, white 1968 Cadillac Eldorado. I pulled out my Colt and laid it on the seat, between my legs, where I could reach it quickly. As I pulled up Sadek and another man in a white jacket emerged and leaned on the car. I couldn't see if Lizzie sat inside through the Caddy's smoked, rear windows.

"So, you made it," Sadek began, when I climbed out of my car with the .45 in the rear of my trouser belt. I felt sure they would also be carrying, heavily.

"Where's Lizzie?"

"And I am rather interested in the whereabouts of *your* hostage? Please?"

"Alright. Wait a minute." I walked to the boot of my car, unlocked it and cut through the tape around Altay's ankles with my knife.

"Get out," I told the foetal fat man. Helping him out and holding the barrel of my Colt .45 against the small of his back, I told him, "Walk slowly toward your brother when I tell you. Stop when I tell you, or I shoot."

I marched him around to the front of the car and shouted, "Here he is Sadek. Now the girl! I have this, so no funny business." I waved the Colt and he nodded to the man in the white jacket, who opened the door of the Cadillac. Lizzie stepped out, looking tired, but she seemed unhurt.

"Are you okay?" I asked her. She nodded.

"She's quite alright Mister Andrews." Sadek nodded again to his man, who brought Lizzie around to the front of their car. Both Sadek and the other man drew pistols, Sadek aiming his at Lizzie's back, the other man, at me.

"On the count of three!" I said. "One, two, three…"

Both Lizzie and Altay walked toward each other and passed, about three feet apart. It looked like Altay wanted to try something, because his brother shook his head and the fat man walked on, stiffly. When Lizzie reached only a few feet from me, she suddenly rushed into my arms.

"Oh, Jason!"

"It's okay honey. Stay calm. This isn't over yet."

I was right. To cut a long story short, Chico attempted a takeover. With two of Sadek's men paid off, he was able to get the upper hand briefly in the ensuing gunfight, but the addition of Altay's marksmanship meant a stand-off.

"You get all the drugs!" Chico yelled "If Miss Stevens Andrews get wasted!"

Lizzie and I had been sheltering from the hail of bullets behind my car, which now looked more like a giant sieve. My shoulders sagged.

"This means Chico's debt will be paid off!" I told Lizzie.

Sadek's grinning face appeared above the bonnet of my car a moment later.

"Hey, don't worry. We're not finished yet. Sadek is only after the drugs," I wanted to whisper but of course it would just sound like mumbling. I tried smiling.

Near the Cadillac and Pontiac stood a green 1968 Ford Mustang Fastback, opposite, a grey Ford van. From its open rear doors four men were carrying large sacks over to the boots of the three cars. Two men with semi-automatics guarded them.

As I watched, it became clear the men around the Mustang were Sadek's. Suddenly Chico's men opened fire on them.

I turned to Lizzie and tried to shout. The tape-gag had

become to loosen, so I worked it free by flexing my jaw.

"Turn round!" I shouted to her over the din of gun-fire. I started working on her wrist bonds with my teeth. Duct tape is almost impossible to chew through, but I had become desperate. I tore at it and managed to find a loose end, which I worked on. It began to come loose after I peeled back a twelve-inch length and soon Lizzie's hands were free. Her sharp nails made short work of my bonds.

"Sadek! A gun!" I shouted. He nodded. A moment later Carlo tossed my Colt over the bonnet. I caught it and crawled to the front of the car. Chico's head pop up over his car, so I tried a shot. Everyone tried to avoid hitting the cars, the only means of escape, if the police came. I knew if I became caught in the middle of a major drug delivery and there was my presence at the killing of Sadek's man in the alley-way, neither looking good in an insurance claim, to say the least. My shot missed. I tried five more shots, but everyone missed. I saw one of Chico's men go down. Sadek tossed Lizzie a handkerchief with six more rounds for my Colt and I reloaded. But everything had gone quiet.

I saw my chance and grabbed Lizzie, but almost pulled her off her feet as I dragged her toward the front of Chico's Pontiac We were suddenly hidden from view and I only half heard the sound of police sirens, approaching from the Dump.

"Get in!" I told Lizzie, yanking the Pontiac's red door open. Sadek and Chico fired at us, so I returned fire while she crawled in. Their shots smashed through the right side of the car while I scrambled into the driver's seat, keeping my head below the windows.

If the keys aren't in the ignition we're fucked!

They were there, so I stuck the Pontiac in gear, slammed my foot on the accelerator and swung the car around on squealing tyres to point it down the road to the iron gates. A few shots slammed into the boot, but we were soon out of range.

"You did it!" shouted Lizzie, exultant. She grabbed my arm and squeezed it. "Oh my God. I thought we were dead!"

"We might still be!"

We were hurtling toward the iron gates and they were closed. I could see the police cars and trucks arriving in my rear-view mirror and the Cadillac and Mustang were already on my tail.

"Hang on!" I shouted.

A few hundred yards before the gates I veered to the left. The car jolted violently as it mounted the hard curb-stones and wallowed like crazy as I drove hard up the slope. Doing almost eighty when the car left the ground, we sailed over the barriers and then slammed down on the far side. I wrenched the wheel to the right. The front tyres dug into the turf, but the car came around and we roared down the road.

Sadek's men on the gate opened fire. I almost laughed at their pathetic shots and soon we were beyond their range.

"We made it!" I yelled over the roar of the wind. "I can't believe it!"

"Jaso-..." Lizzie murmured.

I looked at her. I saw a neat hole in her dress, over her stomach. As I watched, a little patch of red began to spread out from it.

Oh dear God!

"Okay honey. Hold on."

I turned north at the intersection and headed out of town. I needed to find a doctor, but just before the intersection, I had seen a flash of green and another of brown behind me. Chico and Sadek were still on my tail.

"Jason?" Lizzie asked.

"Yes honey?"

"Do you love me?"

"Yes baby."

"I'm not..."

"Lean back baby. You'll be fine."

She did, but somewhere between that intersection and the next Lizzie died. She looked as if she had just fallen asleep. I wept.

"You bastards!" I yelled at the top of my voice. "Oh what the hell! My life's not worth shit anyway, except maybe as an insurance pay-out! I'm gonna get you Chico."

I longed once more to see the canyons where my father and I had spent our holidays. I set course for the deepest of them all.

"Let's see what you can do baby!" I said to the Pontiac, putting my foot to the floor. When I reached the sharp turn above the cliff, I slowed, to let the Mustang get right on my tail. I drove straight through the barrier. The Mustang's driver slammed on his breaks, but he wouldn't be able to save himself now. I put my foot down hard. As the car sailed out into space I laughed like I haven't laughed in my life!

***

The Steps

My host said Jason is me, but I don't believe him.

The cars and city of Los Angeles all look familiar, even though Robert Lath would never have known them!

On these damned steps again. I have to wonder if I am alive, dead or just dreaming this. But then again, it would be a nightmare, wouldn't it! Ha! Ha! Forgive the jokes of a sick mind. At least I *assume* I am sick. But maybe not.

The steps feel real *enough*! They are made of stone and covered in fine grit; debris caused by the passing of many feet, no doubt. And yet I never hear or see anybody else. What's going on? Where am I? I shall continue to crawl up the steps. I daren't walk, for fear of falling into the abyss to my left.

I often wish, as I crawl, that my hands would come across some small insect. Even an ant would be a relief. Something to confirm that this is somewhere in the real world and, yes, company. I would even give it a name if I could keep it long enough. Yes! A name for an ant. It's sad how desperately lonely you can get, in here, or down here.

He gave me another book to read last night: The Castle.

***

The Castle

Sébastien rose from his bed, pulled a rough tunic over his head and made for the communal family washroom on the fourth level of the castle.

The soft slap of his bare feet echoed along the cold, damp corridors as he turned a corner and reached the door to the large wash room. The stone walls dripped with the condensed steam that crept through the gaps around the rough door.

Oh no. She's in that bath again!

He pushed the door open and walked up to the stone wash basin.

In the lead-lined bath, imported from Venice, sat Éloïse. Her fine, blonde hair had been pinned up on top of her head. Only half of the hot water remained in the tub, the rest washing around the bath's iron legs. Sébastien's feet left little dry patches where he trod for an instant, before they filled in with water from the black flags.

"Are you enjoying yourself?" he asked. "You must be costing me a fortune in firewood for heating all that water! Do you *know,* your mother bathed once per year and *she* was considered *fastidious*! I don't remember your father bathing *at all*!"

"This is the 13th Century. We're not barbarians any more. Besides, its fashionable now. You should try it more often and then you would smell less!"

He ignored the remark, poured cold water from a pewter jug into the basin and dunked his head. He gasped at the touch of cold water but felt more awake. Turning to face her, he stared at her where the high-water mark formed a curved 'W' under her breasts.

Almost as tall as him, Éloïse had an athletic body. In fact, when his arms-master had left him to train alone, she would often sneak in to pick up a sword and spar with him. She had become adept at parrying his fast slices and cuts, but as his sword-fighting lessons and hers on good house-keeping had become more rigorous, it became impossible for them to continue their secret combat trysts.

They had shared the washroom since children so they were used to seeing each other naked. Once, while he visited her room, her husband returned, so she hid him in the closet, from where he watched them making love.

"You didn't look your best," he teased, after her husband had left.

"You try looking your best when you are struggling to conceive under a clumsy oaf like Egbert!"

Now Egbert, at the Crusades, hadn't been heard of for many months while Sébastien's own wife had gone to Spain to recover from a fever after her first birth. His parents were long gone, father killed in battle, mother succumbing during the birth of her third child, Adelie.

He considered for a moment whether he thought her pretty. His own wife wasn't a great beauty, although fertile, and tavern hags were even less so but could be hired for a silver denier for a whole week, so he had little to compare her with. He supposed Éloïse might be pretty, but since only her husband and he had seen her without a veil and the heavy brocaded velvet Venetian gowns she imported, the question seemed academic. Certainly he thought that her eyes danced and that her breasts were pretty, but since most times his thoughts were taken up with issues of warfare and law-making, he had little time to consider such things.

He pulled up his tunic and masturbated steadily onto her chest, absent-mindedly watching the warm liquid glisten on her breasts and belly as it found its way to the bath water below. When he finished, he wrung out his cock, let down his tunic, splashed water on his hands and teased some dirt from under his nails.

***

Effectively Lord of all he surveyed, Chevalier Sébastien de la Severin, a knight who had already been to the Holy Lands before he had reached eighteen, had grown into a tall man. Considered intelligent, ambitious, ruthless when required, he could also be kind when circumstances allowed. Brought up in the tough world of feudal France, he asked for little quarter from anybody and gave none.

However, his household had become a relatively happy one. In accordance with local custom, once his parents had perished, he had taken over as Lord, and allowed Éloïse and Egbert to live in the castle when they married. They spent much time together and their frequent walks together in the nearby forest, ostensibly for hunting, would mostly be spent talking of philosophy and politics, such as came in the spare news that reached them.

On one of these trips, after Egbert had long left for the Crusades and his own wife had gone to Spain, Éloïse caught Sébastien looking strangely at her.

"Go on! What think you my liege lord?"

He didn't answer so she let it go.

However, when she caught that look in his eye again on a later expedition, she decided to confront him.

"I know what you thought? Why not?"

"What?"

"It would be no great labour to me, believe me. After Egbert forcing himself on me my body would not find yours a burden!"

He laughed it off, but she followed him as he walked around the copse, pulling twigs from a fur tree and rolling the soft buds between his fingers.

"It's but a physical act," she said, placing her hand firmly on his wrist.

As they had once done as children he kissed her hard on the lips and then pulled away. She waited. He could see no reason not to. Ripping open her bodice he grabbed her breasts firmly and swung her around to take her from behind.

Since then he had often taken her roughly, without thinking, but she knew the other side to him.

"The more you take me, the more you will like me and grow tender!" she teased. She was right. When the mood took him, he *was* tender with her. Often he would come to her at night and afterwards, they would lay in each other's arms until dawn, listening to the owls hooting and the first baying dogs after the sun poked its lazy rays over the horizon.

Éloïse knew that taking risks, bravery and ruthlessness were required in a Lord of France.

"In the Ancient World, women were once Amazonians! One day," she told herself, "noblewomen too will again become warriors and do many of the things men do, but not now!"

***

In the bath she watched his semen ran down her belly and mixed with the water, infused with pot-pourri and other herbs and spices.

"At least I know you haven't been unfaithful, by its thickness," she said, "but I prefer to see what you have been drinking. I know every hag for lieuex and I don't doubt your scruples when you have been gone not more than an hour this week."

He washed and didn't reply.

"I don't mind you know. In a way, it's a compliment. I'm a noblewoman, but first I'm a *woman* and … *you* can use me. I wish to nurture your confidence."

"I own you."

"Yes, I suppose, in a way, you do." She sloshed water on her chest and belly to clean off the viscous white fluid. "But how much am I worth?" she teased.

Confined, for the most part, to their stone world during winter, they discussed what little art they knew; fashionable clothes, the few paintings that hung on the walls and illuminated manuscripts. One of these, a Book of Days, which Éloïse owned, had been lavishly illustrated with scenes from the bible and everyday life. For Éloïse, discussing art opened up new topics that she could explore with him.

"Am I more beautiful like this?" she said, opening her arms wide and stretching languorously out in the bath. "Or like this?" she said turning over and exposing her back and derriere to his gaze.

"Compared with what?" he said.

"Ownership is a complicated thing my liege lord. If you want to own something properly, you have first to understand it."

"I *do* want to understand things when I own them."

"So?"

"I don't know Éloïse. Right now I haven't time. I have to go and adjudicate over a Judicial Trial by Combat. I'll tell you when I get back!"

"Always ambitious, feeling that you have no time. You haven't changed!"

He left without answering. Éloïse blew bubbles for a moment before deciding she felt frustrated.

***

While talking with Gerome, one of his knights, about the latter's exploits with women, Sébastien had almost revealed the depth of his relationship with Éloïse. With the word 'bed' on his lips he suddenly remembered the ugliness of Gerome's sister. Sébastien stopped speaking and looked into the knight's eyes. He hadn't noticed before how rich were the various hues of brown in the man's eyes and had almost been sucked in by their trusting look. He didn't want to hurt Gerome. Moreover, he could not be sure if other men *did* take their closest to bed.

Perhaps it's not usual.

The thought unsettled him. Back in his own bed that

night, for the first time, he tried to remember how his intimacy with Éloïse had taken its course.

Of course they had always been *intimate*. They were 'amoureux' from a very young age, but after they had ceased sparring together it had been several years before they had shared such intimacy again. During that time, she had grown up and out and now her her feminine curves filled out her gown, just like her mother's had, before she died.

On this particular day, their father, now battle-worn and suffering from gout, rode with his retinue to collect rent from his many poor tenants. Although often invited Sébastien didn't like to go, because there were always thrashings for reluctant or starving peasants in feudal Languadoc.

Sébastien hunted alone for buck that morning, but after checking many spoors, he concluded that none were fresh enough. He returned to the castle without removing his bow from his back. Stamping his boots to clear off the sticky, October mud, he climbed the stairs above the keep's under-croft to the first floor door and nodded to Mecthilde, the maid washerwoman.

Éloïse sat embroidering a gown and singing to herself, in the parlour.

"What did you catch mon frère?" Her soft question had been accompanied by a mischievous smile. Her eyebrows raised when he glared at her.

"Only *you* do I allow to bate me so," he retorted. "I caught nothing! Prepare me some hot wine while I change."

***

In the 13th Century, a nobleman could not expect to marry until his father died. Inheritance normally constituted the only route to wealth, which offered the only means by which marriage was possible for the nobility. Of course, there were always the local whores for enjoyment, but, aged twelve, wine had been almost the only sensual pleasure available to Sébastien, so he drank with gusto.

Entering the garderobe, he raised his tunic to piss into the stone bowl, which had been carved to resemble the mouth of a dolphin.

Father's eccentric taste is everywhere!

He stared through an arrow-slot and saw the lush, green countryside, rolling out to the horizon under a hazy morning sky. The warm wine flowed toward his protruding cock and gave him the sudden jolt of pleasure that always accompanied its expiation.

"Sébastien! I wondered *where* you were," Éloïse declared, putting her hand affectionately on his shoulder. "I was coming to sit with you."

"While I changed?"

"I miss our conversations. Father has been so out-of-sorts since mother's death that I have been fearful to spend time doing *anything I* like. I don't want to anger him. Can I watch?"

She hoisted up her long skirts and sat on the bowl to his left, swinging her legs idly.

"Why?"

Sébastien had stopped pissing.

"I wonder how a man does it. Is it difficult?"

"Ha! *No* … ."

"I mean to … aim?"

"No. Look." The warm jet rose to the end of his cock and forced itself out in a yellow arc of fluid that went to the centre of the bowl.

She stood stood up and gripped the end of his cock. He stopped pissing, exclaiming:

"What are you doing?"

"It feels soft. I thought it would be hard. You must take care of it, keep it clean. I hear bad things happen to men who don't!" Éloïse stuck her tongue out and he pulled it with his free fingers. She rested her head on his shoulder while he continued to piss. Casually tapping her index finger on the yellow jet of fluid, she hummed in time with her tapping and noted how the arc changed when she tapped.

Sébastien took his hand from his cock and let her control it. His affection for her extended to a desire for her to be happy and explore life fully, as he knew her curiosity demanded.

"What's next?" she said as the last drop fell from the end of his cock, now slightly distended.

"Just shake it."

She followed his instruction and then he started to drop his tunic.

"No, don't! Watch!" she exclaimed.

She clambered onto the other bowl and lifted her skirts around her waist. He could see a light brown fuzz, which he had never seen before, between her legs.

"What's that?" he said, pointing with his finger.

"What?"

He reached out and twisted some of the fine hairs around his finger.

"*New,*" he said.

"Not new! You just haven't been paying attention. There are other things you haven't been paying attention to as well!" She thrust out her newly grown chest and looked from one mound to the other, grinning.

"Oh those. All women have those!" he said. He returned his attention to the fur between her legs. "Like mine."

"Oui."

"Go on then," he said.

He watched her. She closed her eyes for a moment and then arched over, to look at the tiny yellow thread of liquid jetting from between her legs. It made no sound as it fell to the stone and ran in rivulets along the stone tube to the outside of the walls.

He dropped to his knees in front of her while she

widened the spread of her legs so he could get a better view.

"I sometimes wish I had a thing, like you, to do it with, but then I think that it's not very pretty and I like the way I look." She smiled when he looked up at her. She looked between her legs again and he nodded. She took both of his hands in her own and rubbed them affectionately. "One of the maids told me a peasant girl was caught doing this with a boy and she was beaten by her father with a stick. Do you think father would do that? With me?"

"I don't know."

"We mustn't tell him. You won't tell him, will you? And I won't either."

"No."

Sébastien couldn't be sure, but it seemed like the first time he had felt excitement looking at his Éloïse's body. It also seemed to be the first time they had found secrecy necessary.

When their father supped with them that evening both Sébastien and Éloïse found it difficult to conceal the alliance they had formed. They both did their best to seem attentive and free of guilt or conceit about the moment they had shared.

***

During Judicial Trial by Combat the husband had killed his wife, who had been contesting her claim to property paid for with her dowry. Sébastien needed to organise a knightly contest to calm his nerves; seeing the arm of a woman lying separated from her kneeling, screaming form affronted his senses.

He ordered an arena to be laid out in the meadow beyond the castle keep's moat.

His squires erected a small pavilion beside the long, rectangular arena and placed two seats upon a plinth, under the awning. To either side, long benches were arranged to seat the behinds of all his retinue and visiting friends. Jousts were not yet established as a formal ritual, but Sébastien wanted to hold a tournament to display the training practice his knights carried out regularly. He encouraged his own knights to wear brightly-coloured helmet-plumes, overcoats and a shield with his emblazon; quartered black and white with four blue bosses. The visiting knights had been instructed to wear their own colours.

The crowd's cheers were whole-hearted, acknowledging Sébastien as the lordly and benevolent host he intended to be when he walked to the pavilion and sat in one of the high chairs. When Éloïse took the seat beside him, the cheers muted. These fell to murmurs, which burbled for the remainder of the tournament.

During the first challenge, Gerome engaged with Chevalier Martin de Villeneuve, whose own shield had been emblazoned with a red diamond on a white background around a yellow boss. The choice of weapon had been decided minutes before each fight on the toss of a silver denier; maces, followed by swords.

The crowd sucked in its wine-soaked breath as the two nights lined up at opposite ends of the arena atop their snorting mares. At a nod from Sébastien, a horn blared once and the knights lowered the visors on their helms, Martin's an open-faced helm and Gerome's a Hounskull, or pig-faced helm.

Under the blue panoply of sky, the horses charged down the grassy runway. Éloïse found the lavish men's riding gear enthralling. As he rode, the gold tassels around the hem of Martin's purple saddle blanket rippled like wavelets.

Each knight held back his mace until the last moment and then swung with ruthless determination. Gerome's strike missed, but Martin's blow hit Gerome squarely around the face of his helm. The blow swung him around in his saddle, so that his left leg lay almost along the horse's flanks. He righted himself and at the end of their run, the two knights swung around and charged again. This time Gerome's blow caught Martin behind his head, tearing his helm from his skull and launching him from his saddle so that he crashed to the ground in front of his horse. The animal looked bewildered and nosed the back of its motionless owner.

Gerome dismounted and walked briskly to his prone opponent, kicked the knight's chest once and stooped to turn him over.

"Dead!" he cried, dropping his mace and drawing his sword. The audience, silenced by death, looked to Sébastien, who stood and shouted:

"Victory to Geralde of the house of Sébastien!" He held up his clenched fist and the audience roared its approval.

Though the death had been unexpected, the incident could by no means be considered rare, either in training or in tournaments, and it did not perturb Sébastien. Martin's lands would probably now become those of his younger brother, who would thus be spared the life of a monk. He, at least, would be grateful for the tournament, and a fan for the rest of his life.

Four squires dragged Martin's body away and two more knights faced each other. Theirs would be a contest of the spear.

The knight nearest the pavilion, wearing a helmet decorated in niello, spurred his horse to trot to a position level with Éloïse. He stopped and smiled at her, so she returned his smile politely but looked away, as befitted a noblewoman.

"I do this for you my Lady!" he said, boldly.

Éloïse's mouth dropped open. She looked at Sébastien, whose face hid his affront. Éloïse took this as her cue to berate the knight.

"Indeed! Hmph," she exclaimed as loudly as she could.

A ripple of sniggers could be heard among the

audience. The knight grinned and trotted the horse back to his lane

The knight in niello won his contest, but received a wound to his arm. Sébastien praised him, watching closely the reaction of Éloïse, but she didn't seem the least concerned or impressed with the outcome of the contest.

At the banquet after the tournament Sébastien danced with many women and Éloïse danced with many men. Filled with wine, lavish food, the music of minstrels and the first glimmerings of the European concepts of courtly 'love,' the whole company were having a good time.

A young Lady from Normandy, normally not an area frequented by the fashionable, impressed the other dancers with her light step and blonde, braided locks. But beauty, ready smile and flushed cheeks were the bigger draw for every man who saw her.

As the long lines of women and men interwove in exuberant swirls, Sébastien came alongside the mysterious Lady. Her hand brushed his own and the crafty girl seemed to misplace her footing, so Sébastien quickly stooped to save her from a fall. The subterfuge had been noticed by Éloïse, who consequently followed their every move.

***

At this point in the book, the narrative view changes to first person. But I am on my guard. I believe it's my host's ploy to convince me I am Sébastien. But I am not. He is not like me. He's more, well, arrogant. But I also note that the literary style of these books may be beyond my own skill. It occurred to me that they may be books I once wrote. But I am not so sure now.

***

"What in God's Holy Name were you doing looking at that Norman *whore*?" Éloïse screamed at me that night, after she entered my apartment without knocking. "*And after I brushed aside the attention of that rather handsome knight! He, at least, could provide me with a warm hearth and a life of ease, away from here. If I so chose!*" I dared not say anything for the moment. "What do you see in her anyway? You have your wife, you have me and now you want *her*!"

"But I don't!"

"Don't lie to *me!*"

"I only had a few short exchanges, a few phrases passed, with her. She is … charming … it's true, but I don't think … ."

"No, you never *do*. I spurn a knight, proving my commitment to you, maybe I even, what's that new word … '*love*' you, and the first woman you meet after *that*, you are all ears for her honey-words and flowing frocks. I tell you, you will regret this!" With that, she stormed out, slamming the heavy oak door, which I sometimes struggle to move. Such is the strength of angry women!

During the following day I felt a sharp pain in my chest. At first I thought it must be indigestion, but after a few days it still hadn't gone away. I sought out an apothecary, who prescribed a hot poultice, twice each day, and an infusion made from ale, vinegar wine and common butterwort. It didn't work. I began to feel that something had gone badly wrong with me, a feeling that grew to a fear. I awoke in the middle of one sultry, August night, soaked in sweat and panting for breath. I had a great pain in my chest and a black sense of foreboding, which I put down to the nightmare which had woken me:

A voice had come out of the darkness and offered me a choice:

"In return for life, you must choose one of the potions. One is harmless, and one will eventually bring great sickness." Of course I asked which was which and why I had to choose. "Because it's a game I enjoy! And I won't tell you, even after you have chosen and drunk it. That's the bargain."

I thought about it for quite a while, but the draw of life from death, which I knew had to be my current state, proved too strongly. I swallowed one of the potions before I could change my mind. The voice laughed and receded. That's when I awoke.

Recalling the nightmare, I felt panic. Was it real? Which potion had I taken? Is this why I am now ill? I felt confused and my fear grew from this point on.

***

The second time I remember sharing physical intimacy with Éloïse during adulthood occurred perhaps a year after the first. My father, who had now become gravely ill, felt we were still too young to attend banquets, so Éloïse and I had to watch one from the minstrel's gallery.

Éloïse suddenly pulled my sleeve, so I followed her pointing finger. In the shadow of a large stone pillar, a young man and woman wrestled with each other. She stood against the stone and he pulled feebly at his arms with little white fists while he untied her bodice. When he had reached her belly and her large breasts fell free, he kissed her rosy nipples, whereupon her arms suddenly relaxed by her side. Both Éloïse and I giggled when she put her arms around his neck, gripped his waist with her bare legs and passionately kissed his tussled hair.

"She likes it!" Éloïse said. "I wonder what it feels like."

"Hm. I wonder what they're actually doing!"

"Yes."

We both watched while the couple moved together with harmonious rhythm, up and down. Revellers passed them, but nobody paid them much attention. Suddenly the man's shoulders sagged and he pulled away. For an instant we saw, glowing red in the candlelight, his erect cock, but then he covered it. The woman's fur between her legs, black and slick with something, lay exposed for a moment and I felt myself get hard.

"You like *that*," Éloïse said.

We became separated and when I couldn't find her an hour later, I climbed the long, stone steps, away from the banquet, to our own quarters. I heard singing, so I followed the sound to the washroom door. As my pulse quickened, I hesitated, but banished any guilt or shame from my mind. Éloïse sat in the old wooden wash tub, sloshing her hands gaily around in the water.

She hadn't noticed me, so watching for a moment, drew alongside the bath tub.

"Oh!" she exclaimed.

It was the first time since we were very little that I had seen her completely naked. I felt the thrill of a hunter getting his first view of a new valley. Éloïse leaned back and let her body relax, so that I could take it in. She smiled and her eyes seemed to glow, making me feel like a King. My cock rose between my legs under my tunic and Éloïse watched the cloth move.

"What's that?" she said. I lifted my tunic and showed her my rod-straight cock. "Is it … is that how it gets because you're looking at my body?"

I felt a fierce heat pass through my body and shuddered as the excitement threatened to break over me like a volcanic wave of lava. I dropped my tunic and ran from the room. Some sort of guilt had finally overpowered me. Éloïse later reassured me that I needn't feel any guilt.

***

After I had danced with the 'Norman whore' Éloïse had avoided me for weeks and the bad dream returned with increasing clarity. I noticed a red colour in my piss, a pain in the lower side of my back and feared I truly had become fatally ill. It seemed that I would pay for my love of Éloïse after all.

The memory of the wave of guilt in the washroom returned and the first pang of guilt in my adult life assailed me. As did all nobility, I attended church regularly and confessed but, now, deep inside my unconscious, the first stirrings of unease began their long journey to the need for my first confession about my private affair.

For many months, however, life continued with little change. My book-keeper counted the taxes, which I drew from my vassals and villains, I maintained the castle and the region prospered economically. The pain in my lower back seemed little worse than a riding injury and the red colour of my piss vanished. Then, a messenger came from the East. Éloïse's husband had been killed in the Crusade.

This triggered an upheaval. Of course it wasn't an emotional one, Éloïse had little affection for Egbert and I certainly had none, but I had to consider the matter of Éloïse's future. My position obliged me to find her a new husband. I felt reluctant, of course, but my long-estranged wife's sudden renewed interest in coming home reinforced propriety, so I began the long search. Éloïse rejected every candidate after feigned careful consideration, until it became obvious she would have none. I confronted her and she confessed; she couldn't bear to leave. She begged me to let her stay and I agreed, but with my wife's return, out trysts were, by necessity, conducted more covertly than before. One memory is typical:

My wife had just descended to break her fast in the lower hall, when I found myself walking behind Éloïse, in the same direction. A hound sniffed around us.

"You have to get rid of her!" hissed Éloïse.

"What?" I retorted, barely awake.

"She's not good for you and you know it!"

At a turn in the corridor, I grasped Éloïse's haunches and hauled up her long skirts. She readily bent over and I patted her plump bum while my lazy morning concupiscence hardened.

"I can't get rid of her that easily. It will look bad. Not everybody is as blind as you think, you know!"

I entered her and slid my pizzle right up to the hilt in her easy flesh.

"Hm! You have no guts, that's your problem! I have forgiven you for far worse sins than she ever would. I have a good mind to tell her what you're actually like!"

"What and end up gossiping with a hag over my cock?"

I felt my cock getting close to spasm as my semen rose into it, looking for that way out that would bring me to ecstasy. For the moment, I wanted to stay on this plateau of bliss, so I withdrew slightly, pulling down Éloïse's bodice, so that her breasts were freed.

"Hm! I bet she doesn't look this good, does she!" Suddenly the little spasm of anger left Éloïse and she pleaded, "Oh! Sébastien, it's not that I am jealous, or anything like that really. It's just that I need you. Without you, life wouldn't be so bright and joyous!" I pulled her dress up further to see her waist. I gripped it firmly. "I know what's good for you too!" she said, petulantly. Now I felt angry. I pumped harder into her and relaxed when I felt myself crest the hill of desire. I felt my juices explode inside her and the resulting contentment. Withdrawing, I pulled down my tunic. She evened the plaits of her dress and we continued down to break our fast with my wife. I caught only the briefest flicker of animosity from Éloïse toward my wife, in the briefest narrowing of eyes.

***

The drain of both women on my resources started to tell and Agnès saw an opportunity. She requested all manner of provisions, fine furniture and materials and when I protested, she invoked the approbrium of her family's wrath, an effective ploy since they were land-owning neighbours.

Whether from the fear of cuckolding, or a renewed flame in her heart for me, what brought on Agnès' new purpose, I never did find out. However, she pursued it with some vigour. Suddenly, I found my book-keeper using red ink for the first time in many long years and protesting most fiercely that I needed to find new sources of income. I was in debt!

At the same time, a poor harvest brought on a rebellion by my villains and this had a double-effect on my coffers. On the one hand, I had to pay for mercenary knights to put it down, and on the other, few taxes were being collected and fewer seemed likely in the future. The strain told on my health and the redness in my piss returned. I began to doubt that God could possibly be on my side. This doubt came to head during a visit from Gerome.

"Gerome. Welcome. God be with you. It has been so long!"

"Sébastien, God be with you too. How is your family?" He accompanied the traditional enquiry with a blush.

"Fine. I am about to exercise the hounds. Won't you accompany me?"

We took the dogs to nearby fields, to hunt for hares. While they came and went, we walked and talked. After some pleasantries, Gerome came to the point of his visit:

"Sébastien, there is a matter, a delicate matter, I have wanted to broach with you for some time, years, in fact. I think I can delay no longer."

"Go on. We have always been friends."

"It concerns Éloïse." I smiled disarmingly. "There are … . rumours – they may be unfounded, I know, but they are persistent – that there is something going on between you. A tryst. Are you aware of these rumours?" He countered my stony silence with another approach. "I ask because I think that is what brought your wife, God bless her soul, back and I have heard your accounts are not good. Folk in the villages around her are calling you the 'Devil in the Tower!'"

"Are they really?" I replied, astonished.

"Well, you know they like to gossip, and they probably don't take it too seriously just yet, but Agnès will stoke the fires if she can … ."

"Yes, I see. Well … ."

"No. Not this time. I don't want a circumspect answer from you Lord. I am answerable to the Church and ultimately to Lord God Almighty. I must know … . The *truth*!"

"Really Gerome! You sound like the Inquisitor, come to find a Cathar! I am not such a one." We walked on a few paces and my indignation slipped away, into the loamy soil. "Oh, Gerome, I once almost told you. I cannot directly confess, for I feel I have done no wrong." Even Gerome might well one day betray me, so I chose my words carefully. My relationship with Éloïse could be called Heresy and thus would be punishable by death, if openly admitted. "If I say we are very, very close, would that be enough?"

Gerome paced on, his hands clasped behind his back. "Éloïse is a divine woman Sébastien. I have liked her since we were children. I wouldn't endanger her unless … ."

"Ask no more of me Gerome. You press too hard."

"Ah." He looked at me and our eyes met. He understood the truth then.

He left in an agreeable mood, but his tone seemed full of caution as he wished me to, "Fare well."

***

My relationship with God had never been a truly personal one, but now it became so. For Éloïse's sake, and my own, I began to grapple with my faith.

While pain racked my body, I knelt and placed my forehead against the family pew in the Abbey. For some time, I could not think what to say to God. I clutched the carved wooden back of the pew in front until my knuckles began to pale. Not knowing how to start I decided to say just that:

"Lord God, I don't know where to start. I… I am confused. The first thing to say is that there is something wrong with me … . I am sure … . I have a feeling I am dying. I keep having a dream. It comes with little variation. The Devil taunts me. It is this that makes me think I am dying. The Devil offers me two potions, one benign and one lethal, and I drink, but I do *not* know which I drink. Now, I am beginning to think I really *have* met the Devil and I drank the lethal potion. But then again, maybe it is just a dream and I am a sinful *man*? I have tried to be a man of God, to go to church and be a good Catholic, but there is … something … which I think could be wrong. No, I *know* it is wrong, in the usual sense, but I feel that there *could* be exceptions. I have carnal knowledge of … of Éloïse, who is *not* my wife. There, I have said it! It *would* be sin, but she *likes* it! And I love her. I never intended it to happen, but we are both *so happy* together. It doesn't seem *right* that it can be *wrong*. Oh God, I am not sure what to do. If I stop making love to her, she will hate me. But if I carry on, perhaps you will punish me with death – no, I don't mean that. I mean that my path to you will be full of pain. I am prepared to die, as all must, but to suffer so much for so long, as others I have seen similarly afflicted; that I can hardly bare to contemplate. God, please help me to know which is the right path. And rid me of this wretched dream… and illness."

I sat silently, waiting for the purifying voice of God. It didn't come, but a bright point of white light emerged from the darkness that had been clouding my mind. I knew I had to pull away from Éloïse. The thought seemed as clear as if it were written on a slate so I resolved to do just that.

***

After a sulky, silent meal, a week later, Éloïse asked:
"Who is *she*?"
"Who?"
"You know what I *mean*." She delivered this with such
venom that I sucked in my breath.
Here we go.
"I suppose you mean another woman … again!" I
replied. "I'm not seeing anyone. I wasn't last time and
I'm not this time."
"Well, you seem to be *avoiding me*." She seemed at
once hurt and angry.
"Certainly, Lady, I am not! We have broken fast
together and supped every day this week!"
"You know what I mean?"
"No, I don't."
"You haven't touched me. Usually you are inside me at
least a few times each week." Her brow furrowed.
"I haven't been in the mood."
"You mean you went to the Abbey." I remained silent.
"And prayed!"
"Yes, I did. I am … not well."
"The pain in your back? Here, let me … ." She stood
up suddenly, making, the heavy chair scraping noisily on
the stone flags and approached me, but I brushed her
away.
"It's more than that … ."
"Well, what then?"
"My piss is … . red."
"Oh. Hm."
"It's not usual. I think it's bad. I think I may be dying."
"Don't be absurd! How *can* you be? You're young and
strong!"
"I've heard that red blood in your piss *can* mean *death*.
But that's not what makes me feel that way. A dream … .
I have had a dream, over and over again." I stared into
space. My voice, I realised later, must have sounded far
away while I told Éloïse of my dream, in which I met

Satan. She listened patiently, nodding with pursed lips.

"Just a dream. That's all! Pay it no heed!"

I sat, silently, for a long while. Éloïse must have sensed I had come to the very verge of saying something; the air remained charged with expectation as she waited, silently. A servant came to the sill of the door and turned away.

"I *did* ask for God's guidance. We cannot do it anymore. I am sorry Éloïse." I couldn't bear to keep my glance away from her eyes, which, as I expected, welled up with hot emotion.

"You did what? You asked God's *permission*? And then I suppose you *asked for forgiveness*?"

"Actually, no. Not yet. I am probably too much of a coward."

"You! A coward! That's funny! You are the last man I would consider a coward Sébastien." She shook her head. "I can't believe this! I can't believe this!" She had been sitting, perched on the edge of the chair until then, but now she shot up, like a bolt from a crossbow, and paced angrily about the room. Her long skirts dragged on the flags. "I suppose what we mean to each other, after all these years, is *nothing* to you. I mean *nothing* to you. You didn't even *talk to me* about it. You're a *traitor*! You're abandoning me without even so much as an *explanation*! What we do is *nothing, nothing,* I tell you, compared with what others do; hacking, maiming, stealing. Even the church condemns to death and persecutes." I stared at her, silently, blankly. I had not the energy or will to argue. "Look at you! Oh, I don't even know how I *feel*! All I can say is that every obstacle, we have overcome, together! We have done everything *together*! That's *why* I do it with you. Not because of the simple pleasure; I could get *that* with any stable hand, or any of your noble friends. Do you think I like the gossip that follows me like a starving whelp, biting at my heels? I have given all that I have to you. And now you cast me off, like a … like a … lame mare. No, not even that … ." She was getting into her stride now and Éloïse, when she was angry, was quite a sight to behold. "Like an old bitch who cannot pup anymore."

My eyes closed with the agony of guilt and shame. She knew she was scoring hits. A few more and she might have me. "I don't know if you are dying or *not*, but I do know this; while you are in this world, you may as well have all affection you can get. And I will give it to you. Your illness is nothing to do with what we do, or how we feel for each other. It could happen to anyone. And I say to you; if I had to choose between you and life, or between you and either a God, who doesn't care, or Satan, who does, my choice would be clear. Affection is all we have in this life." She stalked to the opposite end of the oak table and planted her small white hands squarely on the back of a chair. "Well, I can tell you, Sébastien, I don't give up so easily! It's not God who I am fighting for your love, it's Satan!" With that, she stormed up the stone stairs and out of the room. The air fizzled with heated emotion long after she left. I sat there, motionless.

Well, she certainly makes a good case!

***

Now I felt guilty for *not* making love to Éloïse, so we continued, for a while. My wife's renewed interest in me extended to my health, although only for reasons of self-preservation. Without me alive, she had no means of income. However, she rarely ventured out of her chambers and indeed gained weight at an accelerated rate. Her concern about my health did not extend to offering any practical aid to my illness, which took its course, so that soon I began to lose weight and suffered the sweats at night. I had little energy and only Éloïse's cajoling persuaded me to eat proper meals to counter this. I was becoming melancholic, believing that whatever ailed me had to be far-advanced and signalled my inevitable death.

For a while I continued to enter Éloïse as often as before, but soon even that failed to arouse my interest. She occasionally relieved me by hand, although I think it did more to satisfy her protective instincts than anything for me.

"Why do you do this ma soeur?" I asked her one day.

"To keep it in is bad for you," she said.

"Where on earth did you hear *that*?" I didn't disagree with the wisdom, but her worldliness constantly surprised me.

"I just heard it somewhere."

She also often offered me her breasts to suckle, which I dutifully did. But I was slipping away and I knew it.

***

Doubt had entered my mind and infected my spirit. Like a dominant black cloud, it blotted out all other lucid thought, until all my attention became focused inward. The world of physical objects became like a dream to me, no more than passing phantoms while inside me, the battle raged. Of course, I had heard of battles for men's spirits before. Monks would spend months in consideration, a special form of contemplation, and even ordinary men might retreat to a monastery, most commonly at the approach of death. So it would be with me. I had myself taken more frequently to the Abbey where I began to donate more silver denier each week to their coffers and in exchange, monks would pray for me. Though I lay awake at night, listening for the voice of God, I never heard its sweet sound. Instead I frequently found myself facing Satan in that strange, windowless room. The dream gradually became a little clearer:

I would be sitting upon a seat with a tall back in a large room with red walls, although I could not, it seems, see the ceiling. I had the strong impression that a door had just closed behind me and on a plain, heavy, oak table in front of me, stood a large bowl of fruit and two gold goblets. I looked down and saw that I had been clothed in a simple white cotton tunic, which left my legs and arms bare. My wrists bled from what looked like cruel, binding wounds and although I couldn't see my ankles, a similar, burning pain emanated from them. I breathed hard, a cold fear gripped me and inside my head a voice screamed:

"Am I dead?"

On the opposite side of the table sat a shadowy figure, dressed completely in black. The acrid smell of burning wood came from somewhere and a slightly bitter taste lingered in the back of my throat. I opened my mouth and repeated the question inside my head:

"Am I dead?"

The figure moved and from shadow that appeared to cling around him, a cool pair of blue eyes crystallised into a gaze I will never forget. They seemed to crease into a smile, though I could not see his mouth.

"That's a very good question," a voice replied. It sounded silky smooth, infinitely patient and self-assured. "Suppose I were to tell you that the concept of 'life' is all in the mind, that there is no such thing as life or death, unless you believe either?"

"Who are you? Where am I? Am I well?"

"No, you are not well. And I am not going to answer the other two questions." I accepted his authority unquestioningly, so didn't even formulate a repost. He seemed to grow impatient. "This time, you will have to choose quickly."

"This time?"

"Suppose I were to offer you life?"

"But you just said … ."

"You are not … *alive*. Does that answer all your questions?"

"No. I don't … underst- … " I tried to stand, but found that I could not. Some kind of will, like a giant iron fist, held me in place, making my own will seemed as nothing in comparison. With sweat trickling into my smarting eyes I eased back into the chair. "You said you could offer me life?" I noted curiously that the terror inside, when one knows one is dead, is very quickly overcome by the pragmatic desire for life, if there is but the tiniest chance.

"Yes. It's within my power. Don't ask yourself too many questions. Just listen to my offer. In front of you are two goblets. In one is an innocuous drink, somewhat tart, in my opinion, but nevertheless, harmless. The other will kill you, but very slowly. It won't be a bad death, quite stylish in fact … ."

I swallowed. "So what's in it for you?"

"Ah, at last an intelligent question. It's an experiment. For you, it's a good deal."

"How can I believe you? How can I trust you?"

"You can't. At least you can't know for certain."

"You are going to tell me which I have chosen? After I drink it?"

"No." He sank back in his chair. His features faded into shadow.

I considered his offer for a long while before trying to stand again. I couldn't even raise my hands, except to reach toward the goblets. I took both in turn and inspected the content, swirling round the red liquid in both. Remembering what the figure said about a 'tart' liquid, I sniffed the delicate aroma; somewhat fruity. But both drinks smelled the same. I said a silent prayer to God:

"God, if you can hear me now, wherever I am, please help me make the correct choice!"

I had the uneasy feeling that neither goblet could be the right choice, but I pushed the feeling away and took the goblet to my right. Raising it to my lips, I said one last, "Please God," out loud and drained its contents. I felt no ill effects. The drink tasted fruity and tart, as the figure had explained. I sat back and wondered what would happen next. That's where the dream always ended. I never knew whether I had taken the poison or not.

***

As my illness progressed and I became bedridden, I became increasingly angry. An anger greater than I can describe, it seemed an incendiary, black anger; boundless but aimed roughly at whatever, or whoever, had taken my life from me. I felt cheated. More painful than the loss of life was the loss of *certainty* of life, for there could be no peace of mind for me. My thoughts were a seething vortex of endless inquiry, seeking some rational explanation, but I found none.

Strangely, my finances had never been better. With the whispered news that, "The Seigneur is dying," even those who accused me of wrongs, became solemnly silent. Consequently, business resumed at its previous levels and good harvests further increased my wealth. If only I had been able to enjoy the bright sunlight that fills the summers in France!

My last night also became the longest. Each breath came slow and hard, as painful as if a nail had been driven right through me. I nearly closed my eyes and let myself go several times. But Éloïse clung to my hand, as if she could not live without me.

"Tell me a story," I gasped.

"But I don't know any! Alright, I know one; The Story of the Mouse.

"Once, there was a family of mice that lived in a miller's house. He was a kind man, but the mice kept eating his grain.

"The miller tried everything to make them leave, but they were too clever, so he decided sadly that he had to kill them. At night, he often heard them chirping to each other like little birds."

Éloïse seemed to be crying, but I squeezed her hand, so she continued:

"The miller poisoned a jugful of grain and laid it in the most enticing places for the mice. Sure enough, by the end of the week, he had found the body of two large mice and once small one, so he felt sure they must all have died. His wife had to visit her sister one night, so he sat up, smoking his pipe by the fire in the kitchen.

"He had been just about to go to bed when he noticed something unfamiliar, by his feet. He looked down and saw a large mouse, larger than both parents. The mouse was old, and he guessed it to be the last survivor of the family of mice, because it looked sick, hardly moving. The miller knew he had caused the mouse's pain and felt that the creature was visiting retribution upon him, but he decided to take his punishment with equinimity.

"Not knowing what to say to the mouse, he continued to smoke his pipe, uneasily. Every once in a while the mouse would summon up enough strength to move and would shuffle a bit closer.

"The miller felt surprised and upset. He asked himself; everybody knows that animals crawl into a quiet place to die, so why would the mouse want to be close to me? As the hours rolled into those of early dawn, the mouse still lived. Overcome with grief and guilt the miller tried to comfort the mouse, saying, 'There, there. You sit with me awhile and we will meet the day together.'

"In truth, he had only sait it to comfort himself. His imagination ran wild with speculation about what the mouse could be feeling, but he could only guess that perhaps the old creature wanted company at its end.

"Finally, the mouse felt death approaching, so drew away from the miller and crawled into a crevice, but the miller could not bear to let the mouse go. He picked up the tiny creature by its tail, carried it into the half-lit courtyard and placed it on a bower of clover leaves while the the mouse hardly struggled at all. 'You will be comfortable there,' he said. He sat by the mouse until its tiny body grew cold and buried it under a hand's length of good soil."

Éloïse lifted my hand and kissed it. After hearing her story, I clung to life even longer than I felt I could bear, but, eventually, I too had to seek that hidden place. Just before I went, Éloïse spoke to me:

"I sometimes wish it had been I who had died at birth and not my younger sister, Adelie."

I smiled.

My last memory is of Éloïse singing to me while the dawn seeped through the arrow-slit in my chamber.

***

The Steps

I argued with Him that I could not be Sébastien, because I had no previous memory of those events. He laughed and asked if they seemed familiar. I had to answer:

"Yes. Perhaps."

Yet again, he reinforces a doubt and dread in my mind; that I am his toy, his plaything. Perhaps that's why I always choose a tablet when they are offered.

I tried counting the steps today. I say 'today,' for there is no time in here, but occasionally I seem to sleep for a while, so I think of the times in between as 'days.' There seem to be about forty steps before each ninety degree turn to the left, around the gaping, reeking abyss. I don't even know why I am talking to you, or who you are. I just feel your presence, so I talk to you. Is that okay? No answer … . Oh well, I guess you can't object then.

I had a vision, or memory, of Éloïse; she is old, sitting in the castle yard, taking the sun. By the look of her dress and the copious number of jewels adorning her, I would say she lived out a comfortable old age. But I have no idea if this vision is the truth.

***

Right, I have decided to carve my name into a stone step today. I realised I am wearing rags so I searched in the pockets and found some kind of coin. It's roughly made, probably from something like bronze, but it's hard enough to carve rough lines in the stone.

I just finished carving my name. Of course, I seem to have more than one name; Robert before my death in the trenches and Sébastien more recently. I carved Sébastien because it seems more real to me right now.

It seems sad to leave my signature behind. It's the only familiar thing in here beside myself. Still I must go on. Maybe there *is* a way out of here.

I am starting to wonder what life really is. I mean; what *is* the difference between life and death? And who am I really?

Do I even *have* a father and mother? I seem to have many lives. So which was the first?

Too many questions.

I'm *not* Sébastien. But what a priapic sod he is! I mean, I don't judge him, sorry, me, for those moral values or predilections. Times were different then. I have to think of Sébastien as 'him,' or else I will go bloody mad! There *has* to be some difference between him and me, if only circumstance; I am stuck on these steps and he seemed stuck in his rigid society mores.

But he certainly seemed to be some kind of modern-day Priapus, the god with the eternal hard-on!

Most men dream of having an eternal erection. That feeling of power is unequalled in life, walking around with something poking at the front of your trousers and the feeling when you release it and the weight drops, only to be caught and sustained by taught muscles. Which man hasn't dreamed of being eternally *hard*?

It's not just an ego thing either. I am guessing that all men, eventually, want to know exactly what a woman thinks about and feels. We're all sustained by the belief, no, faith, that ultimately women want what we want. Okay, so some men never think of this, but most do. We have watched the enigmatic smile, like a secret sun, that passes over a woman's face when she sees a long, hard cock. We all know the pain of a cock that is not hard enough to penetrate her soft, red lotus lips, that look of disappointment that can end in accusations on both sides. The pain is particularly acute, and the guilt magnified ten-fold, when one has persisted with the seduction. At such times, it seems that a man's greatest gift to a woman must be a rock-hard cock.

Oh yes, a man goes through the faux-guilt of being the seducer, pushing a woman to the act she most resists, says she most fears, playing games, but in in the end, one must come full-circle to the truth that a woman wants sex and expects a man's cock to be hard.

***

Leviathan

"I'm not fucking going down that! You gotta be crazy!" I yelled, pulling away from the open hatch. "Don't anybody think about pushing me either! Six hundred and eighty bloody feet! That's … that's like as high as a bloody skyscraper!"

"Well, if you don't do it, you will never get beyond Cadet Helmsman. Up to you matey!" Shorty replied, lifting the glass bottle's open neck to his scowling lips. Everything about Shorty was a tattoo; gaudy, colourful and in bad taste.

"Give me that!" I shouted, swiping the bottle from his fist.

"Oh-ho! Way-hey! He's gonna do it lads!" Shorty roared. A noisome belch escaped from his gut.

"Now, you *know* what you gotta do," Gooch said into my left ear, while clutching my bicep. "Drink some of that and then do exactly like I say. Like I told you before, brace yourself against this side of the hatch, push off with your strongest leg here." He tapped the lower right corner of the hatch, behind me, with the toe of his boot. "Take a deep breath and go for it. As long as you make it to that panel there, you'll be fine. Gravity will do the rest! Loads have done it and survived!"

"Yeah … and a few have died!"

"Not for years!" His pale blue eyes, in a steely face that perched on his six-foot plus frame, peered down at me with hurt in them.

I had been dreading this tradition. The Leviathan Class ore-carriers were the biggest moveable objects man had ever built, much bigger even than the super-tankers of the late 20th Century. Too heavy to support themselves on land, and too expensive to keep aloft in Earth's dense atmosphere, they could only be loaded on the oceans' surfaces. Measuring up to two miles long, and nearly one-thousand feet from the keel to the top of the bridge, or flight deck, depending on their mode at the time, they were awesome to behold.

Most often used on the iron-ore run from Io to the newly rejuvenated Earth, the Leviathan Class ships were most ambitious Ensigns' dream assignment. They chewed up resources and spat out weary crews, but the job paid well and I had always wanted to get rich fast. That's why I enlisted in the Merchant Service. I could hardly believe I had made the grade, and not only that but been assigned to the flagship of the fleet, when I boarded the Abraham Lincoln on my first voyage to Io. But the moment I knew would come and dreaded since the Academy First Year had finally arrived. We had moored about twenty miles west of the Hawaian islands, an area popular with Leviathan crews for its seclusion and idyllic weather.

I pulled on the lip of the bottle and felt a slug of the hot rice wine spurted down my dry throat. "Jeesh! Hate Saki! Why Saki anyway?"

"Kawasaki innit matey? Japanese ship, Japanese toast! Ha! Ha! Ha! Go on Goochy. Get 'im out there!"

"Okay MacIntyre! You can do it!"

"Thanks Gooch!" I replied.

I stared at the Holy Grail, the panel, five feet or more from the rear edge of the hatch. It sported black scuff marks where rubber of countless heels had tarnished its shiny surface. Like an altar, it had been maintained in exactly this condition for the whole of the Abraham Lincoln's fifteen years in service. I would be the thirty-ninth sacrifice. My heart pounded so loud, now I had decided to do it, that I thought my ribs might split open. If I hadn't been so young, I would have been worrying about a heart-attack.

Shit! Gotta do this and then the easy life of an Oresman will be mine! Easy money, even easier women, alcohol … .

I braced myself with my weaker left hand on the hatch frame behind me, my right gripping the rear frame. I had rehearsed this in my mind a thousand times. I didn't want to look down, but I told myself one last time, "If you fall, the curvature of the hull will take you to a vertical drop and you will fall to your death on the hull far below." Panic crawled up my spine until I wanted to scream. I forced my eyes open and sought for the Holy Grail panel.

If I reach that, it will be a joy-ride! Like the biggest slide in the park! Or pool! But I never went on a slide in a pool! And what the hell is a slide in the park anyway! Oh, what the hell!

Before I could catch my breath or reconsider, I had hurled myself with all the wiry, supernatural strength of youth toward the scuffed, metal panel. I saw the maw of infinite space and certain death whiz by beneath my heels when I swung my left leg forward to join my right. I arched my back and, like a long-jumper, strained every inch of my body into a pleading request for the desired target. In slow-motion, first one heel, then the other clanged onto the shiny metal surface and my heart leaped like a gazelle. From deep within me rose the word, "Yes!" until it filled my whole brain with ecstasy. Finally, my ass touched down and all was sweetness and light in the Universe.

I could do nothing now, but let gravity take me onto the life I head dreamed of. A cacophony of noises assaulted me; the yelping somewhere of a teenage kid, the chaotic slapping of limbs against metal, and the squeal of duretex, crushed between my weight and the almost vertical side of the ship. I could see nothing clearly at first, but my motion became less erratic and I found myself sliding, almost serenely, down the longest slide man had ever invented. I picked up speed, moving soon at perhaps ninety-miles per hour.

"Whoopey! Yeah!"

This is bloody good fun! Yeah!

"Whoo!"

Panels blurred past me and the dark, glassy sea approached like a bottle-green wall. If I had done this right, the flaring curve where the pylon's joined the main hull would slow my descent and I would end up coming to a halt on the rump of the ship. All seemed to be going to plan. I had just enough time to look at the cliffs of Hawaii far to my right and the wide Pacific ahead, but before I could think anything more, I began to slow. My weight seemed to increase as the ship's increasing solidity pressed into my back.

Yes, definitely slowing.

I guessed I was doing ninety again.

I must have been doing one-hundred and fifty, flat out!

Fifty, forty, ten and then I was slowed to a gentle stop. "Jeeeeeesus! Whoo!"

Shit! I want to do it again. No, I mustn't say that! Let's just be grateful I am alive!

I stood up, and waved to the little white dots in the hatch, far above me.

I finally understood how drunk I had become.

***

So there I was; Oresman Third Class, Assistant Helmsman. Half way to Mars I found I could stand the boredom and loneliness no longer. Contract marriages took many forms, but the three most common were seven years, single, short period or single voyage. I hunted through the catalogue of available females waiting for us on Mars, and finally chose the girl for me on the eve of our arrival.

"What do you want to call me?" the ebony haired Asian girl asked, holding a plastic form and stylus.

"What's your real name?"

"Jennifer," she replied, after hesitating.

"Jennifer then."

She ran down the list of questions; did I want her to be submissive, did I want her to be moody or calm, possessive, needy or bitchy? The last question seemed the easiest; did I want the option to extend the contract? It would cost an extra fifty solbucks, now the solar system standard. Like a kid adding something innocuous to a handful of condom packets to deceive the cashier, I didn't hesitate to say, 'Yes.' Perhaps she would think love a possibility. Little did I know I would soon come to love her myself.

As Assistant Helmsman, I spent only about one day in every four on the flight-deck, the rest of the time performing menial duties, like moving cargo closer or nearer to the unloading bays, cleaning, and security patrols. The constant blue light in the endless corridors and the constant hum of solid state left me numb of mind and body. Jennifer's warm body seemed the closest thing to sun and sky that I could get and we made love most nights, though not necessarily to climax. I tried to be good to her and she showed her appreciation by doing things that I hadn't checked on the form; cooking, cleaning and giving me the occasional massage. We even watched movies together and played squash on one of the eight ship courts. For a while the relationship worked well.

But we were more than half way to Earth when she tired of the sex and began to find reasons not to permit it. This made me irritable and we fought.

After one such fight, when she threw my glass snow-globe at the green filing cabinet in the lounge, we both sat down, exhausted, to discuss the situation.

"I can't fight you anymore," she said. "Let's work something out."

"I agree."

"What do you want?"

"Sex."

"When? How often?"

"I don't know. But I might want it any time."

"And I don't. Hm … ." She showed a surprisingly logical and scientific approach to the problem next. "I suppose I could take a sleeping tablet or something … ."

I wondered for a moment if her father had been a scientist, or maybe her mother, but I never did remember to ask.

"You mean you would let me make love to you in your sleep?"

"Well, why not. You're a gentleman. I know you wouldn't hurt me and you can't make me pregnant. If you *did* do anything I didn't like, the security cams would catch it."

Cameras were always filming you, no matter where you were on board. It had been in the contract I had signed when joining the ship, but I forgot about it most of the time.

"I'm not sure. It sounds a bit weird and cold."

"Oh. Well, it was a thought."

That night I woke up, as I often do, at about 3 am and went to the sanicube, before returning to bed. Jen had kicked back the sheets in her sleep. She wore a G-string underneath a grey sweat-shirt. Her hips rose to that lovely peak, where the thong chord pinched her skin into a depressed line around the top of her long legs. I gently pushed the sheets further until I could see her foot. She moved a bit and freed her other foot from the sheets, then she curled up tightly like a little child. Her bum's full curves were so enticing that I had to swallow before I could tell myself not to do it. Not yet.

"Okay. I like the idea," I told her over breakfast.

"What? What idea?"

"Sleep. You sleep, I do it and we'll see how it goes."

"Oh, that. Well I will have to get the right pills."

"How about naturally. Just during normal sleep."

"Hm. That *would* be cheaper … . It's fine by me. But no waking me okay? If I wake, then you stop. Deal?"

"Deal."

"Oh and please *do* tell me when I wake, so I can clean myself."

That night I again found myself lying awake next to my dusky beauty. As usual she slept on the left side of the bed, but this time I felt free to try something. I had already turned the heating up a notch, so I pushed the sheets off her legs and this time she didn't curl up. She lay three quarters flat, with her right hip slightly raised and her right leg bent. I ran my forefinger under the chord of her thong and observed no reaction, which turned me on. I ran my fingers around to her buttocks and then put my whole hand inside the narrow piece of silky material that covered the divide of her buttocks. I felt the tiny, downy hairs that grew there for a long time while I wondered how to remove her thong.

Is it better to do it quickly, or slowly? Hm. Quickly.

With one smooth movement, I slid the thong down her right hip, but it stuck. I had to wait a very long time before she turned over to face me and then I found that the right chord had slid up her leg again. This time, I held the left chord down until she turned and then deftly pulled the right chord down, while climbing over her so that I remained behind her, but this time I woke her up.

"Unlucky," she murmured. In the morning she couldn't remember anything of it.

For the next week, I struggled with this conundrum. The solution? Sliding each chord an inch at a time, I found the thong half way down her thighs after a few of her turns. From here, I had only to slide them down and over her feet. She even kicked her feet to help me remove it!

What a lucky man I am!

At last, like a sculptor studying a rock he would soon begin to carve, I could look at her bum without fear of interruption. By the end of the second week, I knew every pore, every hair, better than I knew my own hands.

"I see you succeeded with my thong at last. Well done.

Now at last I can have some peace. But I'm happy for you, honestly. You're so sweet." She kissed me that day and we were friends again.

During my duties I had to spend endless hours navigating the cargo decks on the Company hoverbikes. On one such excursion, on Deck 7, something strange happened:

The hoverbikes used a magnetic system developed by the Army on its huge battle-cruisers. Two magnetised strips of iron in the centre of each corridor repelled a similar electrically charged magnet in the hoverbike. On such large ships, such forces were easy to generate from the very disturbance that the ship's forward motion created in space. I had travelled halfway along a corridor, whistling to myself, when suddenly the hoverbike grounded, sending out sparks and me, flying over the handlebars. I picked myself up and, checking for bruises and cuts, licked blood off my forefinger as I walked back to the bike. It still sat bolt upright.

Weird! I can't move it!

After scratching my head, I went to the nearest intercom box and called the bridge. Gooch's soothing voice came online. "What's up MacIntyre?"

"Ah, Goochy. Something weird's happened. My bike's got stuck! It's glued to the floor! What the '*ell* has happened to the magnetic system?"

"Sounds like … . Wait, we haven't seen anything up here. Wendt? Seen anything?"

"Nope but it sounds like a vortex to me. We get them sometimes. It's usually bad news for *someone*."

"Get your ass up here Mac. I want you and your girlfriend on the bridge at the double. I want us all together while we talk this through. I've heard of vortices, but never experienced one. They're *bad* news, if they're for real."

Jen met me on the bridge. "What's happening," she said, bleary-eyed. Her t-shirt had been pulled on hastily and clung to her breasts tightly, revealing her nipples. All the other crew-members stared at them. Jen didn't seem to care, but I did.

"Haven't you all seen a girl before? Stop *staring*!" I yelled

"Hey! Cool it, MacIntyre," Shorty replied, glaring. Most of the crews never had females on board, because they became Oresmen for the money, and women, especially on long voyages, only spent it. "Little Oresman thinks he's the bees-knees cos ee 'as a *woman*! Wait till you see your bank balance at the end of the voyage little un!"

I felt like kneeing Shorty in the groin.

"Okay. I been reading online all the websites about these vortices," Gooch began. "There's a lot of waffle, but seems to be a few common traits. Shorty, you say you've been through one once. What was it like?"

"Not nice. Not nice at all. It's just like an area of non-normality in space, whatever that is. They don't stay in one place. They drift. I don't think any bugger understands them, least of all the dome-heads. The only sign of them is magnetic. Apart from that, they are invisible. What I *do* know is that we lost half of the ship and one crew-member. And another went mad."

"Lost half the ship?" I prompted.

"Nah. Not like you think. It was a small freighter, so it didn't make the news. The company that owned it wouldn't want *that*. Basically a large part of the starboard side of the ship … *distorted*. It kinda melted. I can't explain it much better 'n that! The engine on that side was useless. All the systems had to be re-routed. There were leaks all over the place. It took days before we could go off oxygen tanks and we lost one crew-member. He was in there at the time, in his bunk. All we found, after cutting for days, was a lump of flesh and bone that you couldn't recognise. It could have been anything. Except for the *eyes*! Never forget those."

"You said one went mad?" prompted Gooch.

"Yeah. Over the next few days, one guy – Daryl was 'is name – ee went completely nuts. He was close to the centre of the ship at the time. Just couldn't remember his own name, then couldn't remember what 'e was doin'. Then he became a vegetable. I remember the company was generous with compensashin' for the family."

"I read that, in the worst cases, whole ships are believed to have gone missing," added Gooch. "It's all a bit vague though. No scientist will put his name to the phenomenon. Still, we should be careful. One thing I have learned in the last ten years; there is a lot of weird stuff *out there*!"

I shuddered and looked at Gooch. He gave nothing away. I looked at Jen, but she chewed gum nonchalantly and smiled. Nothing seemed to phase her.

Over the next few days, the Abraham Lincoln suffered failures of various systems, near to the corridor where the bike had become stuck. The ship was so vast that none of these failures were terminal. Each time, we found a backup system we could use, or a new route for the wiring. But the crew became more reluctant to go near that part of the ship. Then the phenomena stopped. Everybody felt on tenterhooks for a few days, but it soon became clear we were through.

"Let's celebrate!" I said to Jen, coming back to our quarters after a shift.

"What? The vortex? We're *through*!"

"Yes. What shall we do?"

"Let's get drunk and watch a movie. An old classic."

In fact, we watched three movies, while drinking that awful cheap green Ionian wine, so popular with young kids these days. I hadn't thought of Jennifer as 'young' until then, but she showed her age but setting the n-gen to make the wine.

We fell asleep, tangled together on the sofa, and I remember that we had been laughing our heads off about something, just before we slept. Life felt good again. Eventually, cramp forced me to wake her up and lead her to bed. As usual, I woke at around 3 am and for the first time since the vortex arrived, I felt like sex.

I used the well-tried technique to ease off Jen's thong and waited. When she turned over, I could take my time looking at her pussy, shaved into something like a classic 20th Century 'Brazilian.' She looked lovelier asleep than awake, but while studying her pussy very closely I noticed something odd. I saw, written in tiny, black letters, the word, 'Hello.' I smiled at her cheek.

"You little wench!" I whispered. "Hello."

The sweatshirt proved much harder to remove! I did consider cutting it off after a week of trying, but Jennifer's collection of sweat-shirts were her pride and joy, so I had to be bold. That night, when she turned to face me, I slid my hand up inside her sweatshirt, until it reached her armpit, and then gently pulled her elbow into the sleeve of the shirt. She wore man-sized shirts, so this wasn't difficult. However, she did stir, so I had to kiss her and whisper her name over and over again to calm her, until she mumbled something and went back to sleep. As she turned again, I pulled her lower arm and hand through the sleeve and waited for her to settle with the sweatshirt half off. I then had the simple task of repeating this for the other side, so that she ended up with the garment only wrapped around her neck.

I decided that to make an attempt to pull this over her neck would have to wait for another time. I just wanted her *torso* naked for now. Most women don't wear bras in bed, but Jennifer did, or at least she had, since our new rules had come into effect. Perhaps she wanted to set me a challenge, but of course, releasing her bra strap at the back offered no great challenge.

I had more difficulty removing the underwear. I kissed her when she turned onto her back and she stopped rotating. She seemed to have an itchy nose, but, while she became engrossed with this, I simply pulled her shoulder straps down her arms while she obligingly held them up and even seemed to find it funny. There she lay, revealed completely to me. Jennifer was, for an Asian girl, quite well-endowed, but I wouldn't say she was bigger than an English B-cup. Nevertheless, her breasts were very beautiful, so I kissed them wholeheartedly.

I noticed something black under her right breast.
What the hell..?
I had to push her breast up to see it.
Writing!
I couldn't read it until I turned on a sidelight. This disturbed her, so had to quickly turn it off, but not before I had seen what was written there. "It's been a long time Davie." A cold tingle ran down my spine, because nobody except my mother called me Davie, I didn't allow it.

It's just Jen being cheeky!
But I didn't feel like going any further after reading that. I rolled on my back and stared at the ceiling. Memories of my mother came unbidden into my mind; images of her pushing me on a rotaswing, chasing me around the garden, pulling faces at me when I had cut my knee. Eventually I must have fallen asleep.

Before I left for my shift after an n-gen meal of eggs, sausages, fried bread and bran flakes, Jennifer spoke to me, holding a cup of coffee between her two, well-manicured hands. Her gaze seemed far away, which made her seem a lot older.

"It was lovely, waking up naked this morning. Thank you. I feel ... loved."

"Really?"

"Um hm. I can't explain it. I feel ... complete." I nodded. "I can wear something, *specially* for you, if you want?"

"Okay. That will be nice. Thanks Jen."

"Who?"

"What?"

"Oh. Sorry."

"It's okay." It was an awkward moment, but I didn't have time for a discussion.

"Bye," I said, and left.

***

I wondered about this exchange during the day and, as sometimes happens during relationships, a prick of paranoia pierced me. I called up Jennifer's record online again and read through it in the cold light of day, or at least the artificial light of day. Although I found no sign that she used a fake name, something I had suspected, I did notice something I missed the last time; she had an ultra-high psychic rating.

Hm! How could I have missed that?

I wondered if she might be a very sensitive woman. I thought that might explain her lack of interest in normal sex and her interest in 'sleeping sex.' Perhaps I seemed too insensitive during normal sex. I, however, had begun to feel uneasy about the sleeping sex, that it was wrong, even though consensual. I had felt the ghost of a guilt from the start, but her consent had made me push that to the back of my mind.

I met Shorty in the canteen.

"Are you alright MacIntyre?" He put down his tray and sat next to me. Shorty never does this and he *never* talks nicely to me. His pale green eyes peered at me, as if I were shrinking.

Something is very wrong.

"I'm fine. Why?"

"You sure? Nothing … odd happening?" An image of Jennifer at breakfast, confused, flickered into my mind, but I killed it quick.

"Yeah. Nothing odd. Thanks for asking though. How are you?"

"Well, I'm fine son. Fine. Nice of you to ask." He seemed to relax and tucked into his meal. I, on the other hand, felt very uneasy with this bully eating next to me.

What can he want?

"How do you feel about religion?" he asked.

"What?" I felt dumfounded. "You're a believer?"

"Well yeah. Not much o' one, but I
pray … occashinally."

"Well, now you ask. I'm a Christian. A bad one. I haven't been to church since I was a teenager. I believe in God though. Always have done."

He nodded slowly. "S'just that some say those vortices are made by the Devil. Personally I have come to the conclusshin that it's a hole, a space empty of God. Mebbe he just can't go there, I dunno … ."

"Hm. Why d'you say?"

"Oh nuffin."

***

On my way back to our quarters, a funny thing happened, funnier that Shorty talking to me in the canteen. Goochy gave me a project! We do this once each month. It's supposed to be educational. He knew I would be too nervous and had always let me off. Now I *had* to do one, on vortices!

Bummer! Like I am really interested? And anyhow it's gonna take hours to research it.

***

I have just spent two hours researching vortices and you know what? I think I know now why Shorty talked to me. I *also* think he talked to Goochy and got me assigned this little project. Most of it is just hearsay and stuff about technical defects discovered on ships, but then I find that a number of sites I want to look at are blocked! And it's not the usual Merchant Service firewall either! They are coming up as having *illegal* content, which is weird! *Then* I find this site, run by an organisation calling themselves the Church of the Christian Wave Functionists, which at least I could access, probably because they are considered too crackpot to be a threat to anyone. So I read their articles and find that they have a theory that the vortices are encountered where Wave Function breaks down, or at least where the Wave Function is anomalous. The CCWF point out that, in each case, where a vortex has been encountered, one, and only one, person has died. In *each* and *every* case!

That's weird! Their conclusion? The vortices are some kind of battle ground for a soul, and therefore part of a religious battle. Heisenberg would probably have a fit!

I must admit, the boys are gonna shoot me down when I present this little lot. It should promote some discussion though, which is Cool! I never thought I would enjoy making a presentation!

***

Last night Jennifer slept in a man's white dress shirt, over her bra. I slowly, carefully unbuttoned it, noticing that she had generously covered her body with an exquisite fragrance, like spring flowers under the noon-day sun. I couldn't help pressing my nose against the flesh of her belly, once, after I had remove the shirt. She obligingly turned over, so I unfastened her bra, kissing her smooth back where the impression of the buckle remained. She murmured something before sighing deeply and falling asleep again. While she faced away, I worked her thong strap down her right thigh and waited for her to turn. When she finally did, I slid the thong down to her knees and pulled it over her feet. As usual, she gave a little kick to help me, then I pulled her bra straps over her yielding arms. At last my dusky, Asian beauty lay completely naked, still asleep. She let her hand fall over her mouth and spoke to herself, but I couldn't understand what she said.

I wanted very much to make love to her, but I had to whisper to myself, "It's okay. She has given me permission."

I eased out of my briefs and placed my hard cock against her bum. I felt for the conch shell of her pussy and separated her lips. She already felt moist, which reassured me, so I pushed slightly, but she rolled onto her belly! What was I to do? Praying to God that she wouldn't wake up, I whispered that I loved her and put my hands under her belly. I hauled her up until her haunches were resting on her knees, a most unnatural position for a sleeping woman! I felt sure that she would wake up, my breathing came in rasps and I almost passed out from the tension, but my little Jennifer slept on peacefully.

Thank you God! At last I can have her. She's all mine!

Savouring the moment, I slowly slid inside her and eased forward until the round flesh of her bum pressed against my belly. It felt good to be inside her like this, so I moved inside her, forward and back, hearing the gentle slapping sound of my belly against her bum. Whether because it felt natural, or because it felt like a natural progression, she didn't wake, but only moaned slightly. I felt half way to ecstasy when I noticed it a thin line of lettering, half way down her back. The beautiful, calligraphic sentence lay in the channel of to her spine, which is probably why I hadn't seen it before. I had to put my face close to read it.

'Oui, mon cherie Davie.'

Shit!

My hairs stood on end, but I couldn't stop. My mother often inserted the French 'Oui' in sentences. I felt, knew, my mother's spirit had entered the room. She was talking to me, but I couldn't stop. A million thoughts and emotions passed through me as I climaxed inside Jennifer's body. But was it Jennifer? How could she *know* how my mother talked to me? Nobody knew, because I never spoke of this with *anybody*!

But Jen is psychic? What does that mean? Do I even believe in it?

I spotted another delicate thread of black letters, further up Jennifer's spine:

'Oui. Do it! Do it! It's been so long!'

***

"I don't need to tell you, do I?" I asked Jennifer when she woke beside me when the pre-dawn blue light came on.

She looked down at her sticky groin. "Ha! No, you don't. I see you enjoyed yourself."

"There's something I gotta ask you. I didn't sleep at all last night, thinking about it."

"Wait. Let me just shower."

I had intended to ask her, straight out, about the body-writing, but by the time she came back, I had revised my approach. I smiled and said:

"Something has happened that reminded me of something I saw on your profile, something we never talked about."

"What's that then?" she asked, arch-coyly.

When she sat on the bed I leaned forward and rubbed her nose playfully with my own. "Your psychic-ness."

"Oh. That. Well, it usually freaks people out … so I don't talk about it much. Not now. It was a big thing when I was a teen."

"But your rating is almost off the scale!"

"Yeah, I should be in a lab, I know." Her lovely brown eyes had opened wider and stared into my own. Her face slowly crinkled up in a toothy smile and we both fell sideways onto the bed laughing. I put my arm around her and pulled her face into my chest, whispering:

"My little lab-rat. Jen, the lab rat. Jen, the *psychic* lab rat! Ha!" She snorted with laughter at this. "So what are you really good at?"

"Oh. Reading people's minds … that sort of thing. My mother was a clairvoyant. Do you know what that is?"

"No … I heard the term somewhere. Some kind of

magician or something? A witch?"

"*No-oh*! Don't be silly. She … connected people with spirits … usually their close relatives who had died. It was all very touching. Quite emotional. I was quite good at it too. But I did it by reading people's minds. When my mum found out, she was really cross! 'Don't you go conning my customers! They pay good money for the genuine thing!' she told me. 'But mum,' I said. 'I *can* read their minds!' She smiled and replied, 'Oh, I have no doubt you have talent. But you're not a medium.' Mum seemed to listen for a moment before continuing. 'Yes, I think reading minds *is* your thing. You should focus on that.' So I did, until they threw her into prison for the twentieth time and the cops were after me too. I decided to focus on college and drop the extra-curricular work. Actually that only lasted a short while." She leaned back and stared wistfully at the ceiling. I leaned over, kissed her and lay back too, before saying:

"Well, perhaps that all has to do with what I wanted to talk about … specifically."

"What *is* it then?"

"Well, it's a bit difficult."

"Go *on*. I'm listening."

"Well, the other night – in fact, for a while now, when I have undressed you – late at night … ."

"Yeah." she murmured, snuggling up to me.'

"You had words, sentences, written in neat black letters on your body … ."

She pulled back quickly, not coldly, and looked me squarely in the eyes. "I thought you wrote those? I thought it was really … *kinky*. But I liked it. They're a devil to get off though … ." She added, laughing, "You used my indian ink pen, from my calligraphy set, didn't you?"

"It wasn't me Jen. Honest!"

"Well … then … how?" She seemed very unsure, confused.

"I don't know, but here's the really weird, freaky – no, I mustn't use that word – weird bit. You – sorry, whoever you are that wrote it – called me Davie, several times. Only my mum called me that!"

"Um. Well that *is weird* I suppose … ."

"But wait. She … I mean 'she' because I feel it's a she … used the word 'oui.' My mum used to drop the word into sentences, because her father *was* French."

Jen giggled. "Woo! That's spooky. So you thought you were making love to your mum! Ha! That is so … kinky! Davie! Ha!"

"Now! Now! Don't use that name lightly!" I tickled her. It felt so good to behave like a proper couple. "Yeah, and you know what? Last night, when I was finally inside you, I noticed a small sentence written up your spine, near your hair."

She clutched me like an excited school girl. "What did it say?"

"It said, 'Oui. Do it! Do it! It's been so long!'"

"No! Really? That's really weird." She cupped her hands over her mouth and laughed, so that her whole body shook, which made me angry. After laughing for while, she noticed my silence. She opened her eyes and stared thoughtfully at me. "You know Dave, it's quite beautiful really."

"Yes, I thought that too. But it *is* strange … ."

"I mean; it *is* possible I have connected with your mother's spirit."

"Yes, maybe … . But the writing?"

"Who knows? Maybe I *do* write it. I certainly have enough time when you are out in the evenings. If I do it, I must be in some kind of a trance, because I don't remember."

We left it at that and I left for work.

***

That afternoon the crew's mood suddenly lifted. We

were only three days out from Earth and, not having encountered any further vortices, everyone began to feel we had made it. The ship's catering staff prepared Christmas dinner, delayed because of the crisis, and all on board were invited to the canteen. As senior officer on board, Gooch gave a nice speech and then blew a party whistle. All hell broke loose. People jumped on chairs and tables as champagne bottles were uncorked with loud bangs. Party streamers were popped and crackers pulled. Then somebody had the bright idea to break out a crate of kid's water rifles. They used up all the mineral water in the dispenser and everyone got soaked. Forced, with Jen, into a corner, I took cover under a table.

I had been aughing my head off when I felt an excruciating pain under my ribs. I doubled over, out of breath and unable to speak. I grabbed Jen but, in the chaos, it was a minute or two before I could convince her something felt terribly wrong. She tried to get the attention of some crew-members nearby, but they were too drunk to listen. Eventually she found Gooch, who quickly gained control of the crowd.

They carried me away to the infirmary. Jen held my hand while the stretcher whisked me along the Abraham Lincoln's endless corridors.

The multi-scan machine quickly sent a 4-gigaflop digital image back to Earth where it could be processed and analysed by top disease-seeking programmes. The results were verified by an expert; it was cancer of the kidneys. One day out from Earth I found out I may as well be a thousand light years away, because the cancer had progressed too far. At my age, it seemed absurd.

Cancer! Just my luck!

Jen was very good about it and told me:

"I am gonna care for you. It's gonna be fine."

But she found it hard making eye-contact anymore.

We have taken a hotel room in New York and done the sights. I love the room, which is on the top floor, because the hotel has an elevator and I have always had an irrational fear of steps. One of the things that attraced me to the Leviathan Class ore-carriers was that they had corridors and elevators, but few steps.

This is Jen's first trip to Earth, so I have no trouble keeping her entertained. We could lay on our backs on the rooftop solarium all day watching the pigeons and she would be happy. Actually, I have to admit, I like being with birds, but pigeons are *not* my favourite. Too flappy.

"They are so beautiful!" Jen declared one day.

"They're *pigeons*! We call them rats of the sky."

"Rats? I have seen one. Even they are *amazing*!"

But I had begun losing my focus. I couldn't see things around me clearly anymore, or perhaps I didn't want to. Most of the time I felt morose, but then I would think, 'I've got to make the most of the time before the pain really sets in.'

"You were talking in your sleep," Jen said to me in the middle of one night.

"Was I?" I seemed to have just jerked awake. I was sweating slightly and felt confused.

"I poked you. I woke you up."

"Oh. Thanks. Can I go back to sleep?"

"No. You were saying odd things. It scared me."

"Really?" I turned over, kissed the nape of her neck and brushed her fine neck hairs with the tip of my top lip. "Sorry baby. What did I say?"

"I don't want to *say* … ."

"No. Go on … ."

"Something like, 'You are my toy. When I was growing up I always wanted a toy, something I could hurt and be cruel to, but Father wouldn't let me. Now I have you. Come into the garden David MacIntyre'".

I felt like I had been punched in the stomach. Never very good at remembering dreams, for a long time I had wondered if I did dream. Now Jen had introduced me to one of my dreams, I remembered the rest of it:

The owner of the voice, which wasn't mine, I might add, wore a white toga and sandals. He looked calm and sophisticated. When he led me onto the terrace of a white stucco villa, I marvelled at how much its garden looked like the vision of the Garden of Eden from my childhood. Although it had clearly been cultivated, and there seemed far too much variety for it to be otherwise, it had an unkempt look, as if man had never interfered with it. Hew bade me sit down in a wicker chair and walked to stand beside a table, in front of me.

"You thought you were dead," he stated.

"Yes," I answered.

"You were. In fact, you are, but I offer you life."

He raised his hands to the blue sky above us and I looked into his eyes. They were terrible and red.

"Who are you?"

"Do you want to know? Or do you want life?"

"I want … . both," I answered, after hesitating.

"To some, I could give both, but perhaps not you. Besides, you are much too interesting to give you something so easily. I enjoy playing with you. Five times already we have played this game and each time it's more interesting than the last."

"What game?"

"See those two beakers on the table?"

"Yes?"

"They contain a cool draft, to refresh you."

I reached out to take one, but he stopped me with a raised hand.

"Ah-ah! Not so quickly. There is more to it than that." He walked around the far side of the table, trailing his right index finger along its edge. "I will give you life, but, in exchange, you must take a gamble. You must drink one of the … potions."

"Potions? But you said … ."

"Yes. I must try harder at that. A lot of people have said I am prone to speaking ambiguously. Anyway … one is just a cool draft. The other will be fatal, but not for many years."

"So one will kill me? Why give me life then?"

"Because it amuses me. And one will give you a full, natural life, so I am not being unfair … ."

"Must I choose? Isn't there something else I could do in exchange for life?"

"No. What could you possibly have that I would want?"

"I don't know. I can't remember … ."

"Can't remember your life? I can tell you part of it. I found you in the trenches in the Great War of what people call the 20th Century."

"But I can't remember that."

"You will, in time. So choose."

We argued for a long while. I grew more resigned while he remained patient, as if arguing amused him. In the end I could see I had no choice, or perhaps one.

"What will I feel if it's the fatal one?"

"Nothing. They both taste the same."

"It seems I have nothing to lose." I looked at both beakers. I raised both to my nose and sniffed the red liquid inside. Both smelled and looked identical. Something drew me to the beaker on the right. "I will choose that one."

"Don't tell me! Drink it!"

I swallowed one mouthful, then the rest. The liquid tasted cool and refreshing, just as he had said it would. I suddenly noticed how very black and long was his hair. Black as satin at night, it hung in a braided pony tail, which hung almost to the ground. He had the look of someone who had commanded many men. I sat back and waited.

I can remember no more of the dream. Why I had spoken with his voice, I still have no idea. Perhaps he simply wanted to escape, through me, into this world. I have a pretty good idea who he was though. The Devil.

We have been in our New York flat for a year now. I haven't long left to go. Jen keeps begging me to go into a hospice, but I prefer spending the few days left sprawling in the sun on the roof of the apartment block. For some reason pigeons now calm me. I know they're not doves, but sometimes I can believe they are.

A terrible doubt gnaws at the edges of my mind; have I brought this terrible suffering on myself by making some mistake in my life, a mistake that led to this? I can't explain the thought but it keeps coming. I often drift in and out of consciousness and the world drifts in and out of focus. Sometimes I can't tell which experiences are dreams and which are real? I keep having that weird dream about the Garden of Eden though. When I am not dreaming it, I think about it. There must be some significance, but I can't quite grasp it. I will write more tomorrow, if I feel up to it.

***

The Steps

Well, MacIntyre popped out unexpectedly, didn't he? What a strange story. It must be set in the future, because I still don't really understand what an ore carrier is.

And MacIntyre is supposed to be me again. Of course. And *again* a sexual monster. Deviant, obsessive and compulsive. Perhaps I really am all of these people. If so, am I some kind of psychotic egomaniac? I hardly dare believe I'm so obsessed with sex! Perhaps I should ask forgiveness from whatever god I remember. Then all this will stop. It drives me bloody *mad* to find myself back in this godforsaken hole again!

"Hey! You up there. Okay, I have been bad. Forgive me and just give me some bloody *light*!"

Nothing! I wish somebody would just turn the bloody lights on! I wondered, 'today,' if reality is any different when you can't see it! I mean, does it then become a fantasy? I mean, if you can't see anything, then you are constantly imagining everything, aren't you?

***

I nearly fell off the steps last night! I usually sleep leaning up against the corner in the wall where the steps turn, but I must have rolled onto the steps somehow and then woken up with my legs dangling into space! I don't know why I should *care*. I don't even know if I'm alive. I mean, if I fell off, wouldn't my death be just the start of another life? And anyway, it would be interesting to see what's at the bottom. Sometimes I actually have the urge to jump off. Perhaps that would enrage my captor, whoever he, or she, is. Actually, that's a funny thought. Suppose a previous wife or ex has injected me with some drug that induces nightmares like this! If that's the case,

she slipped up, because I don't suffer from vertigo. If I
did suffer from it, or perhaps even claustrophobia, this
would all be a hell of a lot worse. I seem to have a fear of
steps in my various bell jar existences, but in reality –
have to laugh about that one – in here, I don't. But I'm
rambling.

I estimate that I have been climbing for several 'weeks'
now. That means that if this was a tower, I would have
climbed ten times as high as the Eiffel Tower by now. If it
was a mine, it would be the deepest mine on earth. So I
guess that might mean that this is not real. The other
possibility is that somebody is tricking me. Perhaps they
are moving me while I sleep, back down to where I
started, or something equally bizarre. I am going to carve
a little notch on each first step every morning, to check
this.

It's now a 'week' since I carved my first notch. So far,
I haven't come across a single carved notch during my
climbs, ever upward, to who knows what!

***

I am beginning to wonder if this is purgatory. Perhaps I
have been sent here to consider my sins. Certainly it looks
as if MacIntyre sinned, in a way, and the knight certainly
did, but I can't say that the detective did. But they all
seem like the Greek god, Priapus, weighing his eternally
hard cock against a number of gold coins. Didn't I see
that in a painting somewhere? Perhaps Sébastien didn't
care about money, because he had so much? Perhaps the
others were simply flat broke. Maybe there is something
in this idea? But is it any better to be obsessed with your
cock than money?

It occurs to me now that those Leviathan Class ore-
carriers seem pretty phallic, rather symbolic of being
obsessed with one's cock. And MacIntyre lives inside
one. The castle and the Pontiac could also be seen as
phallic symbols. These thoughts make me wonder again if

they are dreams, fantasies.

Oh, how I long to know how a woman feels, to know whether I have sinned against *woman*. Perhaps that would shed some light on my situation! What does a woman think of a man's cock, truly? Is it beautiful in some strange, demonic sense, or plain threatening?

I feel like I'm involved in some kind of game, a game for which I don't know the rules or the objective. I used to think life was everything, but now I am not so sure. What should I wish for now, if not life?

I am rambling again, easy to do in here. When do I get to eat? Do I even need food? Am I even human? I spent some time, a while ago, trying to remember my true father and mother. I couldn't. This makes me sad. Perhaps warmth has always been lacking in my life. Perhaps I am… I am… something really bad. But no, that is just crazy.

"God! Let me out of here!"

Nothing, again, apart from that irritating echo.

How I wish I had a meal of roast chicken, complete with bread sauce, potatoes, carrots and a glass of wine, or a fast car to fetch a KFC takeaway. What the Hell is KFC? Sounds familiar. Perhaps it's a chemical.

Anyway, to return to the subject which obsesses me right now; what is life like for women? I keep thinking of that eternal contradiction between what women say they don't want, sex, and the disgust and disappointment on their faces when they see your cock is not erect. I never seem to worry about this in my 'lives,' because I am always young. Illness has not crept in yet. But as one gets older, this worry tends to follow you around like a lost dog. Joseph Heller wrote something on that disgust of women. I keep thinking of Ovid's Metamorphosis. Wasn't it he who wrote that the ugly Priapus tried so hard to fuck Lotis that the Gods took mercy on her and transformed her into a beautiful flower?

***

He took me to the library again last night. It always seems so vivid that I am sure I must be awake. But that can't be so, because I awaken back in my own body, on the stairs.

But this time was different.

The first time I visited the library I asked Him:

"Good gracious! So many books! What are the all about?"

"You."

"Ha! That's funny. Robert Lath died in the trenches at twenty-three years old. I had only published three books and seen nothing much of the world. I was a bookish academic and had *relatively little* experience with women. How could all these books *possibly* be about *me*?"

"Read one."

I don't remember the title of that one, but I have been reading ever since. I usually skim them and pick out only what catches my eye, because He never lets me continue with the same book on my next visit. None of them were my books. I asked if He knew I had been a writer.

"Of course. I have one of yours. Here!"

He withdrew a pig-skin bound book and and placed it on a table on front of me. The title read, Extracts of a Medieval Text, Concerning a Friar, by Jaques Renier.

"That's my book!" I exclaimed.

I picked up the book and began to read, immediately noticing the poor quality of its prose.

***

Friar

This text was transposed into modern English, from four 7th Century parchment fragments found in Slane Abbey: Les Cartulaires de Les Abbés de Slane, ed Davies. Slane was the centre of learning in 7th Century Europe, and a favourite for royal patronage.

In his account the famous 20th Century demon hunter, Jack Renier, tells how he hunted down a witch called Genesia. Renier claimed the witch had kidnapped his wife, Rosalind, and taken her back through time, first to the 13th Century and then 7th Century Ireland, to be sacrificed on the full moon. Accompanied by his medieval squire, Uberto, and an old knight, Geralde, Renier had pursued the witch and determined to rescue his wife from a fortified tower at Slane Abbey.

By writing all this down Renier unwittingly left us a rare, first-hand account of an encounter with Satan.

Parchment 1: Les Cartulaires de Les Abbés de Slane, ed Davies.

There is not much to tell of our journey overland. We left Hampton by wagon and crossed Sumorsæte to Weston-Juxta-Mare, before boarding a vessel to take us around the coast to Fiskigarðr. There, we took another ship for Iwernia, modern Ireland.

Geralde had been suffering badly from sea-sickness, so must have been mightily relieved when our captain told us we would soon land.

"At last!" Geralde exclaimed. "Thank God! I can see the lights. I hope they have good beer in this place. What did you say it was called Monsieur Jaques?"

"Dubh Linn." This would one day be modern Dublin.

On the dockside I suddenly became aware of a large

group of street-urchins. For a few copper coins, they told me what I wanted to know; Gena had arrived with my wife, two days before.

My heart leaped at this.

Only two days behind her!

"Where can we bed down?" I asked the children. When I had roughly understood their answer, I interpreted for my companions:

"There is a hostel adjoining the monastery of Baile Átha Cliath!"

I paid for two rooms and ordered two servings of the finest food for each of us.

We discussed plans for the next day next to the roaring hearth. I was for leaving, Geralde for taking a break.

"No Geralde. We can't wait!" I told the old knight

"What, not even one little blonde? Just one little one?"

"No time. We have to go tomorrow."

***

I awoke with a nagging thought inside my head:

I don't know what year it is!

The thought left me feeling disorientated. A faint nausea rose in my bowels and fear formed bile in my throat, a sensation noted by many time travellers.

I had to search the town for my Rosalind. Finding the other two fast asleep, I set off, gripping my sword-hilt firmly.

The settlement, for settlement it still was, of Dubh Linn lay encircled by a pear-shaped enclosure, built up to about twenty-five feet by a ring of earth. Outside lay a deep ditch. The ring had been topped by a wooden battlement, which encased a dry stone wall. I crisscrossed the streets from one part of the wall to another. After almost a nearly an hour, a single chime in the northern end of the enclosure, followed by at least three other mournful chimes around the town, distracted me. Guessing that the churches might be taking their cue to mark noon from the first toll, I headed in its direction. I found a church door, upon which had been carved in decorated Latin and duplicated in runes the name 'Saint Peter.'

A clergyman at the altar caught my eye. He turned when I reached him.

"What year is this?" I asked.

Hesitating for a moment, he then answered firmly, "It is Wednesday, the fifth of November, in the year 672 of our Lord Jesu Christus."

"Thank you. Thank you!"

By mid-afternoon I had not learned anything new, so returned to the hostel. Geralde and Uberto were waiting.

"So you finally decided to get *up*?" I said.

"You had gone, so we made some enquiries about the destination of your Genesia Monsieur" Geralde replied. Uberto look surly.

"Well?"

"Uba?" Geralde looked at my squire.

"She went north. At least that is the word on the street."

"Good work! That's it then! We are leaving now and we'll head north. We'll soon pick up her trail. After all, Gena… Genesia doesn't seem to be trying *that* hard to cover it."

We left by the Ford of Hurdles early in the morning, giving a few of the almost valueless copper coins to scruffy youths to lower the hurdles for us so we could cross at the widest part. Geralde's hangover did not help him across the strange and fragile bridge. North of the bridge, we hired three horses and continued along the Cow Road, the Slige Midluachra.

***

Only a few streams, rustic paths and our narrow track, which wound its way lazily north, cut into the gently rolling landscape. Occasional hill forts could be discerned on brows of hills, mainly by faint plumes of smoke from wood fires that kept their occupants warm. I thought the cultivated fields between vast areas of forest looked very beautiful.

"Cursed rain!" moaned Geralde, "Now I see that it's *always raining* in this wretched country!"

From some travellers coming south, we learned of a rumour about a sorceress in Slane Castle. At last the trail grew hot.

Just before the last embers of sunset went out in the sky, we passed around the foot of the hill to its east and saw the silhouette of a great abbey and the religious college on the top of the hill. A small village huddled around the base of the hill and as we passed through, people came onto their porches to offer us all kind of comforts; food, shelter, good clothing and warm ale.

"No, let's keep going!" I shouted to Geralde. "Up to the Abbey!"

My hasty plan, quickly formulated since we had learned of Gena's direction, had been to enter the abbey disguised as monks. To that end, I managed to acquire two habits in Dubh Linn. Geralde would pose as the knight guarding us.

"Welcome to our little Kingdom of Slane," the abbot said, taking each of our hands warmly. "I say Kingdom because it is of course the Kindgom of God that is in Majesty here, whereas the rest of Iwernia is in the hands of rough rogues who call themselves chieftains! It's my little joke of course but, in truth, we are a haven of learning and civilisation in a tumultuous world!"

His dancing eyes, amid soft, wrinkly features which seemed worn by many generations of laughter, endeared him to me immediately.

"I am Abbot Tadhg." He paused, expecting a corresponding reply.

I introduced our little band and told him my prepared story. While the Abbot considered my answer, Geralde and Uberto studiously sipped some more mulled wine.

"Not too much for the boy!" the Abbot said, pointing to the ceiling with his index finger. "If he is to study here, he will need to learn abstinence too." He paused and added, "Royalty from all over the civilised world send their offspring to be educated here."

***

Only two things of interest happened in the Abbey; my visit to the scriptorium and to the garderobe.

One evening after another fine meal I sought out the scriptorium. At the Abbot's invitation I took it upon myself to do some research, so pulled down various weighty, leather-bound volumes to read by candlelight. A bestiary in particular absorbed me.

I found a chapter each on wolves and serpents in the heavy book. The wolves were of many kinds, including shape changers, some good, some evil. Curiously, there were a few, colourful illustrations of winged-wolves. The section on serpents, naturally longer, given its association with evil and temptation, contained illustrations of winged serpents. Neither chapter told me much, but the illustrations strengthened some of my own ideas and theories. By the time I had finished the candle had burned down almost to the rim of the candleholder and my eyes were sore. I found my way back to the dormitory down dim, echoing corridors, but stopped off at a garderobe on the way. The second interesting event occurred while I sat there:

With the cold night air blowing at my bare bottom and genitals, I couldn't help overhearing a conversation that amused me. Two monks, using, as all men do, any excuse to break the rules, were deep in hushed conversation:

"It's not the same now."

"What do you mean? The food's good. I find it very agreeable."

"Yes. The *accommodation* is good. But the learning

leaves much to be desired. There is not the rigour there used to be. But you are too young to remember the previous Abbot, Cathal. Now *he* was a deep thinker. Is, I should say."

"Why? Is he still alive?"

"I think so, although he must be an octogenarian by now if he is. He will be in the Hermitage, down by the river, if he is still alive."

"So why did he leave? Was he thrown out?"

"Nooo! Don't you know? It's a sort of tradition here. When an Abbot gets old, he often retires and goes into contemplation."

"So he didn't do anything wrong then?"

"Well … ."

The conversation went on but I left to find the dormitory.

Parchment 2: Les Cartulaires de Les Abbés de Slane, ed Davies.

"Tell me about the Tower?" I asked Geralde, while we walked back down the hill, after being thrown out of the Abbey. Uberto had already found out that Gena held Rosalind there, so Geralde had gone to scout out the fortification. I hadn't had time to speak with him since Genesia had persuaded the Abbot that we were enemies of the Abbey.

"You should see the main fortification," Geralde began. "It's a tower, part made of stone, and about four storeys high. It's on the brow of the hill, perched on a high mound, to the west of the enclosure. The undercroft is of stone, the corners of the next floor too, but the rest is of wood. The top of the first floor is in shadow, because the third floor overhangs it, and there are … I don't know what you would call them – skirts – around the edge of the base of the third floor, which hang down perhaps five pied … ."

"So it's going to be tough to get in." I concluded. "But I have an idea. There is a man who may be able to help us and he lives somewhere… around here." I turned off the path, onto a damp track beneath some willows. It had started raining again.

"This had better be worth it!" Geralde muttered.

Aha! Here we are!

I stopped and surveyed a rough wooden building, set into the hill. As two-storey tower sat on top of what, I assumed, must be the Hermitage. The bank on the right rose level with its pointed roof. To our left, on the south side, I saw a single story construction and directly ahead of us, a single, heavy oak door with a hinged, iron ring.

I walked straight up to the door and swung the ring against the door.

I heard no reply, so tried once again.

"Nobody here," suggested Geralde. "Come on. Let's go. I can't see anything for us here!"

I twisted the iron ring and pushed on the door. It creaked open.

Very little light came from within. The place seemed to drip with damp and much of the woodwork had taken a green sheen from lichen or mould.

"Come on," I said, stepping inside. I put my hand on the hilt of my sword. Inside I could dimly see, beyond the tower, a nave, whos single candle cast strange shadows upon the walls.

To my left, just beyond the oak door, a few steps led upward, and just beyond those, more steps led down to a stone archway. The floor and walls, to the height of a single course, were of stone.

I couldn't see anybody in the tower, which seemed completely hollow, save for a single rope hanging from a single bell high overhead. The smell of horse dung came from the stone archway to the left and I thought I heard the snort of a horse or donkey from beyond.

Only one option remained. I climbed the few steps to

the other door and lifted the latch. This seemed so
intrusive that I almost turned and left, but with a deep
intake of breath, I pushed the door gently. I watched as it
slowly swung open with two 'creaks.'

"Ha! Who are you? An Angel!" a deep, booming voice
rang out from the darkness.

On a pallet bed, lit by a single, tiny candle, lay a man.
Reclining against the far wall, he leaned on his elbows
and appeared to be in a state of shock, which was hardly
surprising.

"Don't be frightened!" I said. "We are not robbers. I'd
just like to talk with you. We're travellers and I've heard
so much about Abbot Cathal!"

"Eh? Are you *mad*! Anyway, it's just Friar Cathal now.
But please tell me; who are you, for you have the light of
an angel around you. I was dreaming a dark and strange
dream just now and then I awake and saw you at the foot
of my bed. Pray, tell who you are!"

"I'm no angel. But I do think we might have a lot to
talk about. Are you the Cathal that writes books?"

"The same. Yes."

He still seemed frozen to the spot.

"Can I fetch you some water or something?" I offered.

"No. No! No, it's me who has bad manners! Forgive
me." He quickly threw aside some dirty looking blankets
and stood up. A big man, taller than Geralde, he wore
only a light undergarment, which reached half way down
his thighs. For a religious man he seemed not the least
bothered by his immodesty. His grey hair hung in little
strands from a bald head. I couldn't tell if he had been
tonsured, because I saw no hair anywhere on his head, but
for the very outermost fringes above his strongly-featured
face. I noticed, when he passed me holding the candle up
so that we could both see each other clearly, that his eyes
were blue and gave away a piercing intelligence.

"I don't have much!" he shouted, disappearing down
the steps and through the stone arch. He came back

moments later, cradling a large, round loaf of bread, a segment of a round cheese and a stoneware jar. Placing them on one of the stone steps, he went to the altar and returned, carrying three, gold communion cups.

"It's not much of a place I know, but I like it. It has few stairs. I never did like the steps in the Abbey. I have a lifelong fear of steps! I don't know why. I shouldn't use these cups of course, but then that's why I always keep a few spares! Is it raining outside?"

Geralde, who had kept silent until now, answered quickly, "No, but it will shortly."

"Ah yes, it usually *is* raining here. You noticed! Ha!"

He seemed delighted with everything.

"Bring the other things outside. We may as well enjoy some fresh air!"

He led us around the south side of the tower, to an overturned stone pillar, lying in the ferns a few yards north east of it. Ancient runes carved into its stone face were of a type I hadn't seen and couldn't decipher, but seemed to be from a time long forgotten. We sat on the pillar and ate the hard bread and cheese. Cathal uncorked the jar with a very full set of strong, healthy teeth and poured us each a glass of an amber liquid.

"Ah! Very good," Geralde said. "Like one of our strong wines, but better!"

I tried it too. It tasted pungent, like ale, but sweet, and had quite a kick to it.

A single drop of rain fell onto the tip of my nose.

"I think we'll have to go inside," Cathal declared. "It looks like it *will* rain and heavily. It's the only thing that bothers me about this beautiful country!"

We gathered into a circle within the nave.

"We have come from afar, seeking one who has abducted my wife," I began, boldly. "A few hours ago I met a man in the hostel who praised your qualities as Abbot of the monastery, and as a thinker, so I want to ask for your help. Believe me, I wouldn't do this if I wasn't desperate. Short of raising an army, I cannot see how to continue with the rescue anymore!"

"An army! Do you know my son, that thought has been in *my* mind ever since I was forced out!"

"You were *forced* out? But I thought … ."

"Retired? No, that is the way it's *usually* done, but in my case, I wasn't *ready* to retire."

"So what happened?"

"Well, the Prior, Tadh, was my deputy in those days, but not chosen by me. He had big ideas and, *unfortunately*, my fondness for a drop of the sacramental liquid proved the lever by which he was able to open *that* door!"

"Oh, I see."

"But that wasn't what made me angriest, and not what I want to raise an army for. No. That has more to do with Cairbre, the Chieftain. He's a very bad sort and communes with Satan. His followers too, in my view. There is a young woman … ."

"Genesia?"

"Ah. I see you have met her."

"She's a sorceress."

"Yes. She is." My candid statement seemed to astonish Cathal. "I see you are not only some kind of holy man, but a very experienced one, and candid. A most unusual combination!" He refilled my cup.

"You might call me a witch-hunter. Genesia is the one who has kidnapped my wife, Rosalind. I don't know why and most of all I don't know why it has to be here, but I have been told that she will try to sacrifice my wife at the next full moon. That's tomorrow night. I gather it's some kind of magic ritual, but I intend to stop her! I just don't know *how*. I think they have Rosalind in a wooden tower on top of the hill."

"Ah," Cathal said.

Geralde and Uberto had visibly relaxed since hearing Cathal's woes and the knight now grunted his endorsement of each statement of the facts.

The rain outside had begun to hammer on the south walls and the roof of the tower.

"Where exactly did you say you were from?" Cathal asked, after being silent for a long while.

"Ah, well that might take a long time to explain."

"Well, I could possibly help you, but I would need to know a lot more about you. If I act now, it will be the boldest move of my life. But then again, my life so far seems to have amounted to very little, so perhaps the Lord is ready for a little boldness on my part. Why don't you stay the night and we can discuss it at length?"

Uberto and Geralde nodded vigorously their approval of this suggestion.

***

"I was dreaming of an angel with wings, just before you arrived," Cathal began, a short time later. "But there was something strange about this angel. It was a wolf."

We had accompanied him in vespers and followed this with supper, much the same as the first meal, but supplemented with some roast pork.

I shifted my feet uneasily on the stone floor at his question.

"There's a lot to tell you Cathal and a lot to ask. I have many questions and so far, I've met nobody who can answer any of those questions. I hope to find some answers and I hope you can help me."

I told him the story of my life battling Serpents straight out of the Bible. He listened patiently while Geralde and Uberto accompanying my story with many 'oohs' and 'aahs.'

I concentrated most on the vampire serpents, for these were what what I wished to discuss at length.

"I have thought about this much," I continued, "and I now believe the powers of the Serpent I fought were further diminished, because he had used a time portal to reach that battle."

"I knew it! An Angel! You *are* an Angel."

"Well if I am one, I'm a very strange one. What kind of Angel needs a portal to travel through time and has a mortal span?"

"But you can travel though time! You are from the future. Time is no barrier to you!"

"I catch witches. I sometimes hunt werewolves and Serpents. At least, I follow runours of them, but I have yet to see one." I replied

"Yes, that *is* a bit unusual for an Angel, but don't you know Satan spends more time trying to tempt holy men than he ever does rascals?"

I felt deflated by Cathal's enthusiasm.

"Can we have a fire in here?" Uberto asked abruptly, shaking from the cold. "I don't like to ask, but surely there must be a fire of some sort?"

"Of course! I forgot. I don't feel the cold anymore," Cathal replied. "In the stable you will find firewood. Down there!"

While Geralde and Uberto set about their task, we continued our conversation.

"You haven't seen my book my son – what did you say your name was?"

"Ha! I didn't. Sorry, we haven't even introduced ourselves. I was so full on my explanations, I forgot. My name is Jack Renier. The knight is Geralde and obviously you know my ward is Uberto."

"Ah good. Well, pleased to meet you Jack. As I was saying, you haven't read my bestiary. In it I go to great length on all kinds of lupine creatures, and your *werewolves* sounds just like an order of the winged-wolves that I discuss at length. I see nothing strange about the idea that they are Angels. It's one of my hypotheses."

"But I get ahead or myself," I replied. "I was going to tell you something else … now what was it? Oh yes … actually it's hard to get this all in order as it all relates … . Basically, my theory is that what I call Serpents are basically what have become referred to in my century as 'vampires!'"

Cathal and my two companions looked blank.

"Ah, I see you haven't heard of vampires. Well, it's a name we give to the shape-changers that suck blood."

"Ah, of course!" Cathal said, slapping his knee. "Well, why didn't you say so? Of course they have been around since the beginning of time! 'Lilu,' they were called in ancient Babylonia and later 'Lilith' in Jewish texts. In Ancient Rome there were witches called striges, who transformed into screech owls and drank the blood of men and children."

"You are very well informed! Well I have done some research of my own. You know I said they, the Serpents, appeared every sixty years?"

They all nodded.

"Well my experience was in 1985, when I was in my fifties. There were many incidences, well documented, across France, all leading up to my encounter in a cathedral, north of Paris."

"Excuse me a moment. Can I just ask; what is a cathedral?" Cathal asked, frowning.

"Ah. A very large abbey. They won't be built for another three-hundred years or so."

"Ah. Thank you."

"Anyway, as I was saying, there were many documented cases and so, going on what I had heard of this sixty-year cycle, I checked records for 1925 and what do I find?"

All three heads shook vigorously, though their faces looked totally perplexed.

"In that year there were the two greatest cases of vampire murders in history: the Vampire killer of Hanover, Fritz Haarmann; twenty-seven official murders, and the Vampire of Düsseldorf, Peter Kürten; nine official murders. Both claimed to have committed many more.

Going back much further, there are many such killing sprees at intervals of sixty years, as far back, in Europe at least, as Vlad Dracul, father of Vlad the Impaler and notorious murderer. His name is the inspiration for our most famous vampire character, Dracula."

"But these sound like ordinary men Monsieur? Bad men, but men nonetheless!" protested Geralde.

"Yes. I grant you, that seems the case. But Fritz Harmann killed his victims by biting their jugular vein … ."

Geralde shook his head in confusion.

"Here." I pointed to the vein, throbbing in my neck.

"Ah, that is how we kill sheep and cows!" Geralde said.

"Yes. Well that's how this man killed. It's fairly typical of a certain type of murderer. I don't believe he acted alone. In fact, I think he was imitating someone or *something*."

"But he's still a man!" Uberto retorted.

"I'm coming to that. You see, I think now that the Serpents – I don't know how many they are or how long they have been aroun … ."

"I can answer that," cut in Cathal. "There were originally twelve serpents, brought into being to combat the twelve Angels. But some have been destroyed over the years, some by God, some by Satan himself and a few by Angels on Earth, said to be in the form of winged wolves. God created them for just that purpose." He smiled at me. "Well, I am going to sleep soon. An old man tires quickly you know. I think I can help you Jaques. I am dying, but I would like to do one last good deed before I go."

"Dying?" I asked.

"Yes. I have long had the blood in my piss. It is the sign of diseased kidneys. I have studied Aristotle, so I hoped to find a cure in his books, but it's no use. I have the good-fortune to be of strong constitution, but even *I* will succumb very soon. My death, however, is not my only concern. Recently I have had these visions. I find myself crawling endlessly up stone steps in a pitch-black chamber, from which I cannot escape. I have even seen myself talking with Satan. It disturbs me greatly. I am not scared of him, but in the dreams he offers me the choice of life at a cost. It is the worst type of temptation. But I have spoken enough. I am tired."

"Yes. *We* are tired," I replied.

Cathal continued, "Tomorrow, early, I will go and find a friends of mine, another chieftain. He is a rash man and partial to conquest. He has long had his eye on the community of Slane. In fact, he and I have discussed it over many a barrel of ale, but it has always seemed too great a risk. Now, perhaps, it is worth the risk."

We awoke at dawn. Cathal had gone.

"I like him," Uberto said, over a breakfast of bread and cheese.

"Let's hope he's as good as his word. He may come back with soldiers to arrest us," I added

"I don't think so," Geralde said.

"That's the first positive thing I have heard you say for a long time!" I told him.

***

The waiting for Cathal's chieftain and his army proved a heavy cross to bear. There seemed precious little to do in the Hermitage. After he took Uberto and moved our horses to a safer place, Cathal wouldn't let any of us go out. Uberto returned alone with a basket, covered with a colourful red and green patterned cloth. He placed it in the middle of the chapel floor and went to fetch some wooden plates. Geralde sneaked a look under the cover and declared:

"Eggs! Yes. I haven't had one in months!"

We set to the little feast like starved waifs.

Finally, Cathal returned with two men, the larger and

more ornately dressed of whom greeted me by name and took my hand.

"I taught him his Latin letters, and he taught Donel," Cathal said. "You must admit he learned well! Mathghamhain, this is Jack, a warrior and man of many hidden depths, great wisdom and strange abilities. Jack, this is Chieftain Mathghamhain, a very great warrior, Lord, Prince, and leader of the Four Tribes of Tara."

***

Donel had brought even more food and ale, so we settled down under the tower of the Hermitage to a veritable feast next to a raging fire.

Cathal took out a small wooden box. Opening it, he folded it flat to form the base for a game and placed the playing pieces from the box on the board.

"It's called Fidchell. This here, is the King," he explained, placing a red piece with a copper top in the centre of the board. "These are his defenders," he continued, placing red pieces around it. "And these are the attackers." He placed green pieces around the border of the seven by seven, square board. "The idea is to get the King to the edge without being captured."

"You be King, Jaques," Mathghamhain said. "My army is camped in some woods a few miles south of here, over the river. There is a ford we discovered some years ago. It's only passable at certain times of the day and its location is secret. That's where we will cross when we are ready."

Over many games of fidchell we discussed how we would take the tower. While the chieftain and his men fired the tower, I would rescue Rosalind.

"Your move." Mathghamhain said.

"There. I think I have reached the tower!"

"What! You're right. Well I'll be damned. How long have you been playing?"

"I have never played before."

"Mathghamhain is considered one of our finest players!" Cathal exclaimed.

"The game's name means 'wood sense,'" the Chieftain explained. "We say that it often predicts how real battles will go. It's uncanny. I see that our battle at the tower has good portents."

***

The Chieftain had new information in the morning.

"My spies went south, to the coast. An army is coming. I can only assume that Genesia has sent for them. They will stop at nothing and our tribe will be wiped out if we do not act now. If we take the tower and the whole of Slane tonight, I will send out my messengers. You will see that I will have many more allies tomorrow than today."

"I don't think we'll be staying," I replied. "If I survive and *if* I come out with my wife, we will make for the coast as quick as we can. If you can hold Genesia for even a few days, I will be grateful, and … ." I nearly said 'surprised,' but that would have been an insult to Mathghamhain. " … ever in your debt."

Just before the battle I finally had an idea how I might escape the tower. It involved an unconventional use of the crossbow, so I had no idea if it would work but I had talked it through with Geralde and he had agreed to help me. Then we lined up near the gates to the Tower.

A tear rolled down my cheek.

"What's wrong Jack?" Cathal asked.

"For so long I have been on my own. Now at last I have people on my side. I can't tell you what that means. I almost despaired many times."

"Well, it's not over yet!" he replied.

Parchment 3: Les Cartulaires de Les Abbés de Slane, ed Davies.

It is believed by some that the following extract comes next in the story's chronology. This has been deduced from the frequent mentions of 'Tower,' but many scholars have argued that it is a completely unrelated story.

As I looked down at the slain Chieftain of Slane on the wooden planks of the Tower balcony, a deep voice behind me said:

"Nice work."

I turned and saw a knight, whose purple plume, on a helmet much like mine, enhanced his great height. A niello pattern gave his armour a black sheen. A vertical slit ran centrally down from the eye-slits forming a 'T.' Over a full-length chainmail tunic he wore a black cape, trimmed with black fur and two gold wrist torques, like the previous attacker, in the shape of serpents. I could just make out the pair of fleshy, full lips inside the helmet, as they formed words.

He struck at me, so I parried the blow in such a way that our blades scraping against each other and came to a halt, still touching. Several more blows followed but I parried each one and at last saw an opening. I struck at him, but he proved too quick.

"See that gully?" He pointed with his sword to a length of lead half pipe that extended from a slot next to the Tower door. "It's a full moon. Genesia will sacrifice your Rosalind any moment now. When *Rosalind* dies, you will see her blood coursing down that channel. It will drip into the moat, to be diluted to nothing by the water."

I have to reach Rosalind before Gena kills her!

"All I have to do now is keep you outside just a little bit longer," he said. "It should be easy!"

I intensified my attacks, forcing him to parry and fully engage me. As our first blows rang out, I could find no weakness in him and my spirits began to sink. On and on we fought, but there seemed no end to his endurance. I felt I wasn't even exercising him. Becoming weary myself, I paused to catch my breath. Glancing up at the sky, I saw the clouds swirl about the thunderhead vortex above, just like the one I had seen over the Cathedral that day. It looked like a black hurricane, building in the night sky. Faint glimmers of moonlight around its periphery only highlighted its awesome grotesqueness. My worse dread seemed realised. But with it came the understanding of what I fought; a giant of unparalleled skill and dexterity.

A blow from his sword smashed into my my helmet ring, deafening me and rattling my teeth. Stunned, I instinctively jabbed with my sword in defense and heard a gasp as he leaped aside, but not quickly enough. He caught my blow on his right shoulder, the angle making the sword tip slide under the links and force them away. His soft flesh felt the bite of my blade's tip. I saw him glance at the small wound, pink and starting to bleed. He seemed surprised, so I tried a quick series of thrusts to force him backwards. Catching me off balance, he brought down a slashing blow across my shoulder. The mail links of my tunic broke. The blade bit into my flesh. Such a blow no normal man could deliver. But then I saw a flash in the sky. A crack of lightning followed. The knight stepped back. The rain began to pound, slicking the wooden planks on which we stood.

I became suddenly aware of myself, as if I were out of my body, fighting this huge knight. I could see the whole battlefield, watching our battle on the Tower.

We were two knights fighting to the death under the stricken flashes of a thunderstorm, on the evil Tower.

It could hardly be more surreal, hardly more elemental. Fitting that Genesia should have orchestrated it.

The wet, slick woodwork made our boots slip. I came terrifying close to toppling over the railing, when I ducked out of the way of a heavy blow and his leg caught against the inside of mine. I became aware that this big man was finding it harder to keep a grip on the slippery wooden planks than myself. But my concentration failed for an instant. He feinted a blow to my free left arm and then twisted his body. This gave him the angle to sweep the blow across my chest and cut into my sword arm. I leaned backwards and drove with my feet against a ridge in the planks, to force myself backwards. As I did so I felt his blade strike my upper, left thigh and sink deep into my flesh. The cut had gone too deep for me to feel anything but the cold dread of death.

This is it!

I tried to stand up but fell against the rail.

Just in time I pushed myself back from the rail. His sword bit into the wood where my neck had just been.

While trying to pull it out, the knight's boots slipped, making him fall backwards. His great size and weight worked against him and, though he fell against the sides of the Tower, the planks were too wet to break his descent. Seeing him prone, I drove the sword as hard as I could at a sliver of bare neck, which I glimpsed for an instant, below his helmet.

My blade went right through his neck and pinned him to the wooden balcony. I put all my weight on the sword to pin him there, but he tore off his helmet with an unearthly howl of rage. He gripped my sword blade with both gloved hands and, with a strength I had not imagined, began to force the blade out, first from the wood.

The blade came out of his neck with an awful sucking sound, and blood spurting from his wide wound. I knew he would be dead within minutes, but he didn't seem to know it and began to stagger to his feet. I felt pity for the man, as his neck became exposed and I brought my blade down through the flesh under his helmet. My blade sank so deep that the bones in his neck separated and he slumped forward. I pushed him with my boot and his limp body keeled over.

"Dead!" I said gasped.

Short of breath, I forced myself to the door, and entered the Tower.

I saw flames from an iron fire-basket and heard the scream of a woman.

"Jaques! You've come at last!" a dark-haired woman said, looking at me.

I knew her name and I uttered it.

The other woman screamed "Jack!"

The first continued, "I'm glad you have come. But you know, I couldn't do it. The full moon has passed and I *just couldn't* do it!" She looked downcast.

"Genesia!" I replied. "What are you doing?"

"Jack! Is that you! Oh God, what is happening?" the other woman said.

"Rosalind. Darling. I have come for you. Didn't you know I would?"

"Oh God! But … ."

"She's terrified, poor woman," Gena said. "I must say, Jaques, you have good taste in women. I mean, if I am presumptuous enough to include myself. She really has a lot of fighting spirit! She caused me quite a lot of difficulties!"

"Rosalind!" I said again, letting the yearning that had so long driven me be heard in my voice!

"Well, she's not *that* interesting!" declared Gena!

"Shut up Gena. You've done enough damage. I'm taking her and don't think you can stop me!"

I hadn't much time to take in my surroundings. To the left of the door, in the corner of the Tower, I saw what I wanted; a staircase.

"I don't want to stop you Jacques." Suddenly Gena feigned frailty. Ever have I had to be watchful against her guile. She has the power to seduce any man that will listen to one sentence from her uncouth mouth. Her hood had been cast off and her raven hair framed the beauty of her young face in the glowing firelight. "I tried to do it. I want the eternal life, but to take your wife would make you hate me forever. I just couldn't do it. You see, I love you."

I stood up unsteadily and walked over to where Rosalind, wearing a blue gown, had been strapped by her wrists to a wooden bench.

"She looks quite pretty like that, don't you think?" Genesia continued. "Perhaps we could come to an arrangement?"

I took a knife with a crescent blade from a table and cut the rope from my wife's wrists.

"Come on Rosalind. We're going. We have to get out now! Genesia has another army coming!"

Blood from the deep wound in my leg formed a slippery pool around my feet.

Rosalind seemed too exhausted to resist when I drew her to her feet.

"I … I cannot stand," she murmured.

I slung her over my back and turned for the staircase.

"Wait!" shouted Genesia! "I can't kill her, but I can stop you leav- … !"

She lunged toward me. I twisted and easily caught the hand that held the crescent dagger toward me. Turning her small wrist easily, I put the dagger to her face. For a moment we looked into each other's eyes and hers seemed to say, "Don't!" But it wasn't the fear of death that I saw in them.

With her own fist still gripping the dagger, I ripped her dress down from her neck until she was naked to the waist. Her breasts looked as beautiful as ever. I slowly drew the blade across her belly twice, cutting into it the sign of the Holy Cross. Blood poured from the wound and dripped on the floor. She fell to the crude boards, covering her own wound with both her hands.

"I thought you had more power than that," I said.

As I carried Rosalind up the stairs I heard the last of Gena's words become a confused murmur:

"Jaques. Don't leave me… I…"

I struggled up two flights of steps and pushed open a wooden hatch over my head. We emerged into the torrential rain, under a black sky that looked like an upside-down cauldron of boiling sea.

"Can you stand Rosalind? Please try!" I let go of her and watched her cling to the railing edge around the roof of the Tower.

I waved my arms and an answer came when a crossbow bolt thudded into the woodwork below the railing. The wall had been solidly constructed, so the bolt fully embedded itself in the wood, sticking out of the internal surface by an inch.

I reached over and started pulling on the thin line attached to the bolt, but I hauled for what seemed an age, until my fists encountered a knot, heavier hemp rope and a second knot in the hemp. Pulling the rope over the parapet I untied the short length at the end and tied the end of the longer length around the protruding head of the bolt.

"Come on Rosalind. Hang on to me!"

I passed the short length of rope over the main line, wrapping the ends around my wrists. We climbed over the parapet and down to where I could stand on a ledge. I leaned forward and let the rope take our combined weight. For one sickening moment, I thought the rope would break, but we came to a tumbling halt on the wet grass, where I lay, gasping for a while.

We turned onto our backs and found Mathghamhain and his brothers looking down at us.

"Jack! You are safe," the Chieftain declared. "What a great day! If I never live to see another like it, it will make me a legend for all time!"

"We must get away fast Mathghamhain, but before we go, where is Cathal?"

"You must hurry Jack. He has not long. Come with me."

Held up by the Chieftain's own arms, I hobbled to a small crowd just under the trees. There lay Cathal, flat on his back, gasping for air. I stooped over him.

"Ah! Jaques. You made it! I knew you would. Where is this wife of yours we have all suffered so much for?"

I beckoned Rosalind forward and some of the Chieftain's men carried her to Cathal. In the torchlight, she looked even more beautiful than ever, her brown hair once again flowing like little waves around her face.

"Ah, the lovely Rosalind!" Cathal said.

"Rosalind," I said. "This is Abbot Cathal, who has made all this possible. Without him I could not have saved you, or at least not so quickly!"

"You young rascal!" Cathal said. "This is no time for jokes." He coughed twice. Blood spattered his chin. "Took a nasty axe blow to the gut. Serves me right for wanting to learn first-hand about war. Friars should never meddle with war. That's another piece of wisdom I have added to my long list. Still, I prefer a quick death to a lingering one. Oh and Jack, I have to tell you something. Come close."

He was still a strong man and easily pulled me down to him with his hand around my neck.

He whispered in my ear, "This world is not the only world. I have lived before and may live again. But I fear it."

"Why?" I asked in a whisper.

"In all my lives, I have been impatient. I had read all the books in *this* world before the age of twenty. But perhaps my thirst for knowledge, previous to this life, took me too far, brought me to a dark place. I may have become weak and bought life at a great cost to my soul. I told you I had a choice. There were two potions. Both gave life but only one gave life without a long, lingering death. I fear I took the wrong one. But worse, I fear I made a deal with the Devil. There, that is my confession."

He released me and fell back.

"Oh, and its Friar Cathal, my lady, not Abbot," he continued. "So, Jack, I have to ask you one or two questions before I go."

A tear rolled down my cheek, not just at Cathal's bravery, but his indomitable spirit.

"Go on. I will answer if I can."

"What is the future like? Tell me a little of it?"

"Well, what can I say? People are no happier, perhaps, but there are amazing things to see. Men fly in craft called aeroplanes. People travel the length of a country on a long train, towed by a machine powered by steam. In fact, it is quite normal to go on a holiday for two weeks using one"

"Incredible! Flying you say? But what is a holiday?"

"It's a day when people don't do any work. They simply have fun. It's … oh well it doesn't matter."

"Amazing! I could do with a few of those myself. One last question; is the world Christian?"

"It is mostly Christian. But there are other religions; Islam and Hinduism, which are both quite popular in the East… ."

Mathghamhain tapped me on the shoulder, so I looked up at him. When he shook his head sadly, I looked at Cathal's face. It had relaxed into a smile, but there was no life left in it. I took his head in my arms and cradled it, tears welled in my eyes for this man who had made everything possible, everything from nothing.

After a while I stood up. We had to leave. I looked at the Chieftain and saw that he wept silently too. As I looked around me, I saw that each and every person present had been deeply affected by this dead friar. He was touched by a vision of other worlds, other lives, even if he did talk with the Devil.

***

The Steps

I lay the book down on the table in the library and whispered:

"That *is* my book."

"Yes. But I know you read the bit about Cathal talking with… someone very important. And I think you begin to guess who I am. But are you convinced now? Even in your own book you mention a choice of potions. You must know now that it is real."

I felt shaken. I wanted to deny what the mysterious figure told me, but I couldn't find the words.

"It seems…" I finally mumbled, not knowing how I would complete the sentence. "Perhaps there is some truth in what you say."

I looked at all the books around me and felt hope leave me entirely.

"Do not despair. There are still the tablets. Or potions! Ha! You will have more lives. They will all be documented here."

"And more gruesome deaths."

"I hardly think dying from cancer is gruesome."

I awoke to the sound of an echoing voice this morning. I couldn't quite make out the words. They sounded something like, "Am I?" I couldn't make out the direction either. Did it come from above or below? I felt like running in all directions at once.

"I'm here! Who are you?" I yelled. My words echoed off the walls of the stair shaft for minutes. It nearly drove me insane. I felt as if some monster had asked *me* who *I* was. Then I knew the horror of it. The voice that had woken me up had to be my own. I recognised it.

I *am* going mad! If somebody doesn't speak to me soon, I will be lost inside my own mind. It's a terrible thing; believing you are the only one you can communicate with. It brings back all those doubts of youth. It makes you ask, "Am I alone and is anything real?"

What is real? I no longer know. Seeing and touching something no longer makes it real.

Indeed, I have only recently become aware that I have been wearing clothes. Do you see the problem? My awareness has no reality to be separate from, to be observing. I might have been wearing clothes some… possibly weeks ago, but in which reality? Is *this* reality the same as *yesterday's*? I feel that I'm a puppet on somebody's string, but whose? If God, why is He doing this to me? If the Devil, what does he stand to gain from the torturing of *one*, tiny soul?

My lives are a jumbled mess and I only have their historical period to indicate their chronological order. Consequently, I find 'what I believe' to be different in each life. What *I* myself believe, whoever 'I' am, is another question entirely. Everything seems so confusing here that I really don't know what to believe. And yet if I try to analyse my beliefs in any of my lives, these don't help make sense of the situation. I do *seem* to be Christian in all the lives that I can remember. That much is clear. From what I know, somehow, of Christian teachings, the Devil is bad and God is good. Beyond that, the Devil uses any methods possible to deceive people into losing faith and following him.

So perhaps I am experiencing some final 'trial' before reaching Heaven. Yes, that's possible. Perhaps at the top of the steps is St. Peter's Gate!

But then again, I feel more like a pawn in some game, or at least somebody's plaything. Ha! Ha! 'At least'! Why the hell did I say that? I should have said, 'At worst.' Only somebody whose esteem has sunk to a very low ebb, would say, 'At least.' But it's an easy mistake to make, even for somebody who was a writer…

"I was a writer! Wasn't I a writer?" I shout. I listen to

the echo, "…iter ..? iter ..? iter ..? iter ..?" It's still echoing now and will be for some minutes. God, just the echo is enough to drive you insane. Where was I? I need to stop and have a rest. I've lost track of how many steps I have climbed today anyway. Let me just sit down. That's better. Dangle my feet over the edge. Do I have feet? Yes. I can feel them.

So how do I find out if I'm God's pawn or the Devil's? Hm… Good question. Does it matter?

What I am suddenly doesn't seem to matter as much. I don't really care anymore. Just *where I am* is important. For therein would lie the answer to the most burning question in my mind. I don't really care whether I am a vole, an ant or a ghost. I couldn't care less, as long as somebody tells me *where* I am.

But where was I in my thoughts? Yes, I need some process whereby I can determine whether these steps are God's creation or the Devil's. That at least will give me a starting point. It will be quite a big answer actually… and a step forward… rather than up! Ha! Nice joke.

Well, there are no creatures in here, nothing alive except… me… possibly. If these steps were the creation of the Devil, I would expect there to be nothing else, partly to make me suffer more and partly because he has not the inventive capacity. If there were creatures, they would be so hideous that it would give him away.

On the other hand, if these steps were God's creation, there should be *something* alive in here, even if it were just an ant. One miserable *ant* is all I want! If there was one… But there isn't.

Then it must be the invention of the Devil.

But wait! Suppose God really was tempting me; might he not allow me to experience terrible suffering, to test my faith? Surely he wouldn't let me go to Hell?

Wait a minute! Didn't Dante's character in The Divine Comedy go to Hell, before he went to Heaven? Yes!

Then perhaps it really is possible God is tempting me.

This could be a test! It's all a question of *faith*! But my faith never has been the strongest. Oh I wish I had studied harder in Sunday school.

Yes, that give me hope. This might just be a test of my faith!

***

I heard a voice a few minutes ago! And yet there were no echoes. It said:

"You feel the doubt? Terrible doubt? That is my gift to you. Without that you would have nothing!"

"No, I have my love for those I have known."

"Those are just shadows of memory, nothing more."

"Who are you?" I replied

"You know who I am! Cathal knew."

So it's true. It's Satan, the Devil. Cathal *said* he had spoken with Satan. I feel empty, terribly empty and lost. And what he says seems true. All I *do* have is *doubt*! In a world where nothing seems real, perhaps that is all one *can* have! I am *lost*! I am lost in an Alice in Wonderland nightmare, but I haven't her fortitude. I am truly lost, in spirit even! God forgive me!

But how can Satan be interested in me?

Then again, what did Cathal say; Satan is more concerned with holy men than rascals.

But then I really would have to be some sort of holy man, rather than just an ordinary thriller writer.

For a moment, hope flickers in my heart, but it dies just as quickly. I know I am just a man. How else would I have becomed trapped in this Devil's game? My anger is incendiary. I fear that if I find another soul, I will kill it.

***

Painter

This is the journal of Ariel Schechter: artist:

I have cancer, kidney cancer to be precise. I have been so angry that my councillor has advised me to write this journal. I have never been angry, really angry, before in my life. I am a man of moderate moods.

You would think I must be Jewish, but you'd be wrong. In fact, my great grandparents were Jewish, but escaped the holocaust in Germany with their children to England where they brought up their son, my grandfather, as an atheist. He only just escaped circumcision. My father is a Christian, but named me Ariel after Shakespeare's character. He swears it isn't a joke, but it's not that funny. Perhaps that's why I became an artist. You must have seen my work. The painting that bought me recognition was that one of John Lennon doing a victory V just above Winston Churchill's head.

Journal: Day One

Woke up this morning feeling great, opened my eyes to see the bright sunshine, which had been playing across my closed eye-lids in our Muswell Hill flat, and then remembered that I am dying! It's always like this. Most of the time the 'death' thing, my death, is just a dark spot, like a blind spot, at the back of my mind. But then, something will draw it into focus and my mood will take a nosedive. You see, my 'death' is still an abstract concept to me. I feel no pain most of the time and at worst, just a slight ache around the hips and stomach.

Anyway, this morning Christi, that's my wife, climbed out of bed, over me, and accidentally leant on my shin, putting all her weight on her hand. It didn't even hurt that much, but I snapped at her, "What the fuck!"

"Sorry. I'm still *sleepy*!"

I immediately forgave her. I knew the 'condition' caused my irritability. My therapist likes to call it a 'condition.' I think it's so that he doesn't have to say the word 'cancer!' So stupid... My mind, or rather my journal, might wander at times. Tomorrow I am going to try and structure it by telling my story from the beginning, but there seemed something different this morning and that's what I want to say.

Actually, first of all I have to say this and I'm going to *say it*! I have never done anything wrong and I don't deserve to have cancer! There, I have said it. Now, as I was going to say:

This morning I heard a crow cawing. We live next to a park, so it wasn't anything unusual. At first, I wasn't aware that I was asleep, but then the crow started cawing my name.

"Ariel Schechter! Ariel Schecter!"

I only knew this to be a dream, because everything looked like a Hieronymus Bosch painting and I didn't feel concerned. And you would, right? If you knew it wasn't a dream ... So on some level I must have known it to be a dream. I have always been into Jung, rather than Freud, so stick with me here on my dream analysis. Anyway, so this grotesque looking crow, in this kinda snowy landscape, but with a red sky, comes up to me, stalking along like he was a stork, you know, and caws again:

"Ariel Schechter! Ariel Schecter!"

So I guess I must have said, "What do you want?" or something like that, 'cause then he replies:

"*He* wants to see you. Mr BIG!"

"Oh really. Like ... what is this? I've seen Live and Let Die about FIVE TIMES! Is some black dude gonna rip his face off when I meet him? What is this?" Now I am not a funny man, but I felt pretty weirded out by this crow and that made me scared. And when I'm scared, I start sounding like Woody Allen. Not that I like the man. That thing marrying his girlfriend's adopted daughter seemed pretty weird. Anyway, there followed this whole sequence where me and this crow went to Jamaica and rode an old Routemaster bus and everything, and then the crow suddenly stopped the bus.

"Enough is enough!" he said. "We gotta get you back to the MAN!"

Yeah, I like writing capitals cos it helps me express my anger. You can probably tell I've decided not to try and write proper grammar either. I can't be bothered. After all, it's MY journal!

Anyway, I had a feeling the crow was about to leave me, so I told him, "You walk creepy man." But he didn't seem to care. And he did it! He did that creepy stork-walk and left me. Then the door closed. Things stopped being funny.

"Sit down," a voice like molasses asked. I only saw one chair, a large one with red leather upholstery. I sat in it and felt small.

I wanted to say, "Who are you," but I just stared straight ahead, at a shadow in the shape of a large, elegant man. I didn't even try to make out his features.

"Now," he continued, "I know you're a modern man, so I am going to give you the choice in tablet form."

That's when I noticed a glass on the table in front of me, containing something looking like water. There were two small, white tablets either side of it, on a green cloth, like baize. And that's it! That's when I really did wake up.

***

"I'm sorry darling," I explained, as I sat down to my cornflakes and honey in our sunny, pine-furnished kitchenette.

But suddenly she wasn't speaking to me. Typical! I don't know whether to be grateful when she doesn't pity me, or angry because maybe she doesn't care. On this occasion I felt angry. As any man who has been in a long-term relationship with a woman will know, it's the woman who decides where and when battles will be fought. The only choices I now had were what weapons to use.

Righteousness? Jeez, no! Never to be used unless you are absolutely, in the sight of God, correct. How about abject repentance? Perhaps worth a try. The old faithful; ignoring her too. Can work, but tends to lend righteousness to her argument and prolong the battle. Time is the one thing I don't have. Okay let's try this one; the peace-offering from a friend, combined with an explanation. Should at least win some Brownie points.

"Had a bad dream this morning. Only, not sure if it was a dream at all!" No response. She is still tidying away her own breakfast.

"There was this crow…"

"You *know* I'm no good at interpreting dreams Ariel! And I'm really busy. Can you just call Jay? He might have fallen asleep again."

Ah, a response. Worth continuing.

I leaned back in my chair and hollered. "Jay! Time to get up. I'll come in in five minutes, if you're not up!"

Faintly, we hear "Oh *dad*!"

"You *could* have gone to the door! The neighbours will hear!" Christi muttered.

"Anyway, as I was saying …"

"When are we going to tell him?" I had to count to five after this one. Every chance she gets she asks this and she knows the answer.

"Tell him what? We don't even know if it's really going to happen. I might even recover. Not that you'd care!"

"Oh, don't be stupid. I will even love your corpse."

Ouch. Now, I've really dug level two through to ten of my hole.

"Sorry baby. I didn't mean that." I stood up, went around the table and put my hands around her stomach. I kissed her neck. She tilted her head obligingly. Taking a big risk, I gently massaged her between her legs where her pussy would be hiding below the apron.

"You needn't think *that* will get you off the hook."

"Your joke was *quite* funny, but I know you didn't mean it to be."

"Oh! I don't know how to deal with this Ay. I am trying to skate over the surface. Making a joke is just … well, I thought it would … Doctor Michaels said I …"

I let go of her. "And I'm abandoning you. Sorry, but I just wanted to tell you something."

"Okay. Sorry. Go on …?"

"There was *this crow* … Sorry, I sound angry. I mean; there was this crow! And he took me to this strange guy, who I couldn't see, after the crow and I wandered about inside the James Bond movie, Live and Let Die. Anyway this strange guy offers me a choice of two tablets. There were two glasses of water."

"And you took one?"

"No … Actually, I woke up."

"Not much to go on …"

"Yeah. But it felt real. I mean; I remember every little detail … without even trying. You know how bad I normally am at remembering dreams."

"Well tell it to Pauline."

"Um. Maybe I will …"

"Why don't you try painting it!" she suddenly added.

"Hm."

I think I took Jay to school that day because I didn't have any urgent commissions to complete. I remember thinking about painting my dream. But somehow it faded from view in the deep ranks of priorities.

Day 21

I don't like to write this, but my 'councillor' (if you prefer, you can read 'therapist,' because Pauline seems to believe fear of death is unnatural and I can somehow be cured of it. I'd like to see *her* be cured of it. She is only in her thirties, but I have caught her several times checking in the mirror to see if she has jowls) said I should document the first real 'symptoms.' In the middle of the night I woke with the usual dull ache from around the rear of my hips, but this time I felt a sharp pain, on both sides. I managed to get back to sleep again, but I had to go on the internet first thing in the morning and check up on it. Apparently it's very rare to have the pain on both sides, both kidneys, and very unfortunate. It means my death will probably come quicker. But immediately, I thought, 'There is a silver lining to this cloud. Who wants to suffer pain any longer than necessary?'

I am finishing the last, but two, of my commissions, a portrait using only shades of red for a prominent Labour MP. Apparently, I am de rigueur at the moment. It feels like a waste of my remaining months, or god-willing, year, to be churning out these formulaic portraits. But I need to earn as much as I can for my family. Christi and I will have to be extra careful that she doesn't get pregnant again.

I said I would try and write something of my background. I felt torn between doing a mathematics degree and art. I seemed talented at mathematics at school and fascinated by space. Mathematics won, just. A summer spent trying to get a meaningful job in Art confirmed my suspicion that mathematics wasn't the key to the safe career that my father had promised. I felt heavily inspired by Warhol and Hockney and aspired to the Royal Academy, but ended up at The Central School of Art and Design.

It was 1984. Doubtless the apocalyptic date sent the country into a bout of introspection, but generally times were good. We were an affluent nation and I found myself documenting the resulting optimism in the music world. I went to gigs, perhaps three times per week, and dipped my toes in the drug culture of London. I never indulged

much though; I haven't the confidence to try hard drugs.
A few spliffs were my guilty pleasures. I hid my apparent
Jewishness and I would certainly have been considered at
the liberal end of the Jewish community. I often painted in
monochrome and made photograph-like images of artists.
I plundered the past thirty years of art, so you could say I
operated like a terrorist. I blatantly referenced the work of
Hockney, Warhol, even Allen Jones, and made what I saw
as social statements with them. I guess Banksy's art
would be the nearest modern equivalent. I painted Lennon
a lot in my final degree year. He's a fascinating subject
and when I came across a photograph of him with
Churchill, it inspired my most popular painting.
But that would be a brief moment in the sun during my
early career. I think that's all I want to say for now.
Writing about this makes me feel incredibly tired.

It's funny, I keep wondering what the hell I did wrong
in my last life. I sure as hell haven't done much in this
one. But the funny bit is that I never believed in
reincarnation before. And yet suddenly it seems viable.

Day 27

Had that damned dream again. Only this time it went
on further. Still just as real, although this time it seemed
more like a memory. Now I am *really* bothered by it:

The guy leaned out of the shadow that seemed to
envelop him and I saw eyes that burned me like red fire.
When he looked into my eyes, I had to look away,
because the pain became so bad.

"I won't mess you around," he said. "You are already
dead. You know it in your heart." I found myself nodding.
"However, I can give you *life*!" He accentuated the word
'life' so much that he made it sound like some kind of
drug. I nodded again. "All you have to do is take one sip
of water with one of those tablets. Both will give you life,
but one carries with it a slow, painful death … eventually.
The choice is yours." He finished his last line with a

theatrical flourish of the hand and a smile.

"But why do I need to? I mean, why should I? I am *not* dead! I am alive."

"Suit yourself. We will meet again soon. Now you will wake up." And the most terrifying part is that I *did* wake up … immediately. Even worse, this waking world doesn't seem any more real than that one! I have a session with Pauline on Thursday, so I am going to talk to her about it.

Finished that commission! Two more to go! I don't seem to have any more commissions coming in. I wonder if people know I might not complete their work? Thinking more about Christi's suggestion.

Day 30

Saw Pauline. Almost surreal conversation:

"Hi Pauline"

"Hello Arial. How have you been?"

"Not that great actually." I paused, but of course Pauline remained silent. "Um. I had a bad dream. Er … and the pain has got worse. But the dream … I had a bit of it before and it's *weird*! It seems too *real*. Almost more real than the *real* world! This guy – actually I think he might be the Devil – offers me a choice of two tablets. He says I am dead! He says both tablets will give me life, but one will cause a slow, lingering death. I told him to fuck off, basically…"

"Did you?"

"Well no, not really, but I didn't see why I *had* to make the choice. Erm … ."

"What did the tablets look like?"

"Oh … wait. Let me see. They were small and white. They could have been aspirins! Ha! Ha!"

"Like breasts?"

"Eh? They're a bit small for breasts."

"Okay."

"No, seriously."

"But this could be a longing for your mother."

"Her breasts were definitely bigger than aspirin tablets. All the local boys called her Heifer Shechter, 'cos she is a very busty woman … ."

"And I guess you miss … them."

"No Pauline. No. Listen, this is not about breasts. I wanted to talk about a choice of life and death. You *know*; the *Devil*? I haven't got time for all this superstitious breast-fetish stuff anymore. A few years ago you might have got me with it. But I don't care so much for breasts any more. In fact, Christi and I haven't even had sex for a few months. I would love to say I am just as horny as ever, but I'm not! But this dream seemed *too* real! Do you know what I mean? It felt like a memory. I feel that I have actually been there… and talked to him! And the weirdest part of all of it is that he seemed to know I would have doubts about it. He told me I would wake up in a moment and that I really was dead! And I did wake up! Maybe I have been dead! *Maybe* … I did take a tablet and I just don't remember it yet! Do you see? Pauline? Oh, I see. I have to talk, don't I? Well, perhaps you don't want to talk about reality? But perhaps I will never get over the anger I feel about my own *death*! Perhaps you *cannot* cure me of this!"

I felt the ambient air temperature change. Call it instinct, call it what you will, but the air seemed colder. I felt Pauline to be cast adrift. I *had* her. For once, her silence wasn't control, but confusion. However, she found a buoy to cling to:

"Perhaps the man in your dream … the Devil, is in fact your father."

"Ha! Ha! Pauline, you don't give up. No. And even if he is, on one level, it's irrelevant now. Forget your books, your symbolism. Are you here to cure me or help me?"

I endured a long silence of perhaps fifteen minutes. There was no way I would say any more. After all, the sessions were paid for by the Government. I felt pretty much forced to attend. Pauline seemed equally determined at first but, gradually, a vibration in the air told me she had begun to weaken. Finally, she spoke. Her voice sounded like paper cracking.

"I… I think you have issues. I think perhaps you have deep issues of guilt." Like a pier that jutted out into a raging sea, that would be all we two desperate swimmer saw of the session.

No more words were spoken until Pauline said, "The session is at an end Mr Schechter."

Day 37

I should have known that session ending would be different, because she had never called me Mr Schechter before. A letter arrived this morning. Pauline has chickened out. "Dear Mr Schechter… become apparent to me… some issues deriving from your past experiences… might be impacting on your readiness to cope with your current condition. In conclusion, it is my professional opinion that I can no longer provide you with an adequate service and I am recommending your case to be reviewed in a wider context… Bla! Bla!"

I wouldn't care but I think, despite her clumsiness and ineptness, she really might have stumbled on something. I *do* feel guilt.

I have a confession to make and I can be open here, because I have already confessed to Christi. I told her during my tea break this morning. This is roughly what we said:

"Tea's up Picasso!" she shouted from the kitchen.

"I told you not to call me that. A) I don't like his work and B) he died *old*!"

"*Okay*! Sorry. I bought some Bourbons. Remember? You used to love them… *before* we were married. You only stopped because of your weight…"

"But it doesn't matter now…"

"Sorry." She sat down, and Christi never sat down

during the day. Her cup made a funny scratching sound, like a tiny, wooden saw as she twiddled it between her fingers on the cheap, bamboo place mat.

"It's alright," I replied. "It shouldn't be *you*, feeling guilty all the time."

"You mean *you* have some guilt! Ha! That's a *laugh*!"

"What do you *mean*? I *might* have secrets!"

"You feel guilty when you use the last squeeze of *toothpaste*! That's why I love you honey!" she said, standing up. She walked around the table and pecked me on the cheek.

She spoke the truth, but my honesty is borne of abject honesty, not a lily-livered lack of assertiveness. I always hated bullshit. I had found that the more honest I became, the more my work improved. I took a deep breath.

"And how would you react if I… did… have a lover?" She turned, picked up her empty mug and went to the sink where she commenced washing the mug. Her back was to me. She made no other sound. I swallowed the last of my tea and looked with longing at the Bourbons on a plate. But part of my mind watched *me*, watching the Bourbons.

"Now would be the time to tell me." Her answer came so quietly, so suddenly, that I almost lost it in the air. She seemed to be looking out of the window above the sink. The sun cast a shadow across the pane. I have always loved the way glass did that. It's like being able to see underneath a shadow.

"It was a long time ago."

"It's finished?"

"Um… *yes*!"

"I can't say I'm not shocked." I bit my lip. I wanted to criticize her typically Anglo Saxon indirect speech.

"I feel terrible. I… er… wanted to tell you for years…"

"It's alright darling. I'm glad you told me. Ha! I never thought you had it in you. S'funny, I was only saying to Claire a few weeks ago; I would almost *like* you to do something outrageous. When I married you, I expected *some* kind of dark side… some kind… Oh what's the word? What?"

"What?"

"You're not saying anything." She turned to face me. "You're not looking at me. There's something else, isn't there?"

"No! I mean yes. Claire…"

"Claire knows something, doesn't she?"

I looked at my wife hopefully.

"No! No…! *No! No! No!* It *can't* be!" There fell a silence like a guillotine. My fear spasmed. "Claire? How… could that happen? I mean… how's it even *possible*? With my own *sister*!"

"I… it happened when we went to see Les Miserables. You went to the toilet while we were drinking during the interval. She moved round to let you pass and my hand… our hands… just touched. I felt something but… Anyway she smiled and asked if I was busy the following week. I *mean*, not right away! *Later*! Asked me if I wanted to go to the Hayward Gallery. She didn't even say what was on, but I said yes. It seemed rude not to… But then, as soon as I had said it, I knew something had happened. I *knew*."

"Oh Arial! Anybody but my *sister*! Can't you *see*?"

"Yes." I gulped. "It was *my* fault, not hers."

"I don't know… I have to do the shopping. I think I'm gonna go now. I just can't get my head around this!"

I watched her get ready with panic rising in my crop. I could think of nothing to say, or do. She left.

Day 105

It's hard to write anything. Forget my *life*, I can *hardly* find the strength to tell you about my slow death. I feel as low as I ever have. I thought telling Christi about my affair would wipe the slate clean, would stop the dream. I don't even feel guilty any more. But the dreams continue. The pain is much worse. Sometimes I can barely get out of bed. I am on a constant round of painkillers and have effectively fired my new therapist, Dr Zeale (an appropriate name!).

Both Pauline, and now my wife, seem to have abandoned me in one sense. Even my son seems to have formed a hard shell to exclude me!

Christi has been wonderful about the affair, outwardly, but something has changed. She still holds my hand, kisses me and encourages me in bed (to no avail) but something is missing. It's as if, rather than attempt to forgive me, she has settled for delaying any emotional response until after I am dead. I would definitely have preferred the first, but any attempt to broach the subject meets with a cold, insistent distance.

In my dream I know I *did* swallow one of the tablets. There seems to be an *age* between the elegant man's offer and my decision to take one. Usually, I simply reach forward, take a tablet, place it on my tongue and wash it down with the liquid. But it always seems too simple. Last night I found myself focusing on any detail I might have missed. I remembered something:

"What happens if I don't choose?" I asked

"Then you will remain dead. You will have no more lives."

"Lives? You mean I've had others?"

"You will remember them… soon."

"I must admit, I enjoy living, but if this is death, it's not so bad."

"No. This is not death. You will remember that too, soon." I could see him more clearly now. He wore a long, red coat, made of a thick material, like crushed velvet. His hair, black as night, had been pulled back around his large skull, as if by a pony-tail. I didn't trust him, and yet his words seemed to hold untold depths of truth.

"Will I know which tablet I have taken; the bad one or good one?"

"No. And I will not tell you. That's the deal."

"No. I don't think I *can*!"

"Oh, come on! You *have* before. I grow tired of this game. I tell you what; if you make your choice quickly, I will take you out into the garden and we can smoke a cigar together."

"Ha! I know that technique. A friend of mine was a salesman. It's called fast-closing; I can't make a decision so you give me an easier decision! Nope!"

"Okay. *I* have more time than there is in *your world*. But perhaps this will jog your memory."

Into my head came a vision of myself lying dead in a World War One trench. At first I could only see liquid mud in the trench, but then I could make out a muddy arm. What I first thought an oily white rag materialised into my bloated face. My eyelids were pulled back over protruding eye balls. I knew it was me, I don't know how. I knew it was real. I could taste the rust of a muddy death in my throat. Suddenly it seemed miraculous that I could even talk. I felt grateful for… something. I picked up the tablet on my right, placed it on my tongue, took the glass and washed down the medicine. I would live again.

"Good. Now let's walk together," my jovial host said. I followed him through a door behind his seat, down a long corridor and through a pair of glass doors onto a veranda. Before me stretched a fertile chaos of trees and exotic plants. The scene reminded me of an overrun plantation. "This is what *you* call the Garden of Eden. Would you like a cigar?" He indicated a plate on a table. On it were two cigars. He took one, bit off the end and lit it between his teeth. I recognised his red coat as a smoking jacket. I was walking out on a 19th Century plantation with its owner. I took the other cigar and lit it.

"What are you going to do in your next life?" he asked.

"I don't know… I think I'd like to paint."

With the word 'paint,' I woke. Only it felt like going back to sleep again.

Day 115

No matter how hard I try, I cannot think what I have done to deserve such a painful death. My mind refuses to accept that it is fair. Unless there is something worse than my affair with Claire.

The truth is that I have a new feeling, worse than the fear of my own death. It's doubt, terrible, lingering, festering doubt. It's the doubt that I *ever* had any control, that I *ever* knew what I was doing and that I know *anything* about anything. In fact, it's an indescribably deep doubt. It feels like one of those oubliette things; a dungeon that you might never escape from. I never thought I could feel like this. It claws at my back like some Biblical monster. Judaism has always been an easy religion for me; you get circumcised, you avoid certain foods, you have weird haircuts, drive Volvos and go to the synagogue. Then you are a good Jew. Easy! I never had any doubt. Now I do. It's not fair.

I tried painting my dream. After all, I only have half a commission left to complete. None of my usual clients thinks I will live to complete another work. Anyway, I tried forgetting the normal rules. I just wanted to paint with feeling but, to my horror, the final result kept trying to be a painting of pure black, a portrait-rectangle of pure black. I stopped myself before the final stroke and started again. But the result would have been the same. The more I try to paint detail, the less I can see and the blacker the vision becomes.

That bastard refuses to take shape! He must be the Devil!

I hate him.

And now I have remembered something worse, just like he said I would. Before my usual waking dream of the tablets, I had another dream. I dreamt of a never-ending staircase. I crawled on it and never reached the top. My hands and knees were bleeding before I woke from the dream.

At first I didn't connect this with the other dream. In fact, I didn't even remember it until climbing the escalators at Kings Cross one afternoon. Now I'm sure they're connected. They have the same lingering reality about them. Perhaps there *is* some kind of reality other than the one we see everyday.

All this fear (beyond what even my Woody Allen sub-character's can cope with) has led me to search myself for any hidden guilt. I'm not sure it even counts, but the only really daring, erotic thing I ever did didn't hurt anyone. I hope my putting it on paper I might finally exorcise the demon:

It happened at an exhibition of Paul Cezanne in the Tate Gallery, about 1994. I felt an air of expectancy outside the exhibition on that hot, summer morning. I know Cezanne for his bleached paintings of the sun-baked French landscapes, like infra-red images. I happened to be behind an Italian mother and daughter. The mother wore a dowdy skirt, shirt and overcoat and gave the appearance of a plain-minded woman. Her daughter clearly wasn't! I guessed her father must have been quite wealthy, because she wore an expensive, powder-blue three-piece. Blonde, round-faced and very pretty, her body's puppy-fat still thickened her limbs, but not unnatractively. I would put her age at about sixteen.

As we reached The Bathers, the atmosphere became charged. The mob seemed excited. They chatted about the paintings, which radiated a summer sexuality that I found intoxicating. It seemed that only the two women and I were silent.

The girl dropped back behind her mother, so that her ass came close to my hand. I had the urge to touch it, to place my hand flat against the ripe curve of one of her buttocks. I moved my hand closer, but the queue moved and she followed. She turned once and half-smiled at me. I felt that she knew what I wanted. Perhaps the dry, hot paint had imbued her with ready-wisdom, great age and a woman's appetite? I wanted to know.

I felt my erection grow hard, while I followed them. Like two, meek cows, they allowed themselves to be herded. I stayed so close that I could smell the girl's delicate, flowery perfume. As the crowd pressed in around another version of The Bathers, I found myself almost pressed against her Italian ass.

"If you don't do it now, you will regret it forever," I told myself. "But she might not like it. I might get arrested. You won't get arrested. She's young. She will worship the sun."

I turned my hand round and placed it flat against her buttock. She made no move. She didn't pull away from me. I looked down and, yes, my hand really did lay firmly on her ass. I felt as if my cock would break. I felt as if I would pass out. I am sure my face had turned red. I *felt* flushed. She moved her ass, to see the picture better, or so it seemed. She must have felt my hand, but she remained, standing firm. I thought I saw her steal a glance at her mother.

We moved on, so I had to remove my hand quickly. The crowd thinned, but I stayed with my lovely pair of cows. As we walked, I saw that they completely ignored me. They talked over me, chatting of girly things, if I came between them, as if I were the girl's father. Then, I *knew* that the mother had become aware of me. Why didn't she stop me? Pull her precious daughter away?

We continued on. I heard them discussing the paintings in low, Italianate tones. Their voices murmured like clear stream-water over stones. Both looked at each other, not at me, and yet their glances held on to me. I was there. I knew I was *there*! But where? What did they want of me?

We came to a large painting while few others were in the room, and those with their backs turned. I decided the time had come for a decisive move. I loved the mother. I loved the daughter. They both stood together. I moved up behind them like the father, the husband, and placed one hand each on their asses. The girl continued talking. Only the mother flinched for a moment. A glint in her eye showed me her surprise. I held my hands there for an instant before removing them. It seemed unlikely the fire could get any hotter. I thought I would cum. But I didn't. I had now had an erection, a very hard erection, for nearly an hour. I felt I myself to be bursting like a fire hydrant in the movies. Surely this could not go any further. They were leaving. They wanted me to follow. I followed them to the till.

The girl studied a postcard or two, so I placed my hand reassuringly on her ass again, to encourage her. She seemed to take strength from this and chose not to buy. I followed them out into the lobby. They stood in a corner, debating what to do, before sitting on a bench. I sat between them. They both looked at me before continuing their conversation. They seemed to be discussing food. I wondered what would happen if I followed them to the canteen. I wondered if I should go home with them. Or was this just a dream? I wanted to test its reality, so I decided to speak.

"Are you hungry," I asked them.

The spell broke. They stood up and left. I withered and fell into the depths of the bench's support. I could not move for an hour.

Day 116

For the life of me, I cannot see that even that experience was so wrong that I deserve this kind of punishment. But even my latest confession has not released me from the persecution of the dream. I have never hurt anyone or had any deviant sex, I have loved my parents and been faithful to my wife and have not been over-ambitious. I can't see why I have been singled out for this.

I am close to being bedridden by the pain now. Any kind of movement involving bending at the waist is excruciating. I keep getting out of bed and walking in the mornings, just to fight the threat of incapacitation.

Yesterday, I took Jay to London Zoo. I thought he might be too old for it, but a news article prompted the trip and he became quite excited; we had often intended to go when he had been a child, but somehow never managed it. Jay might be the last one to reach out and touch me.

While we both drank Coke outside the little café, he suddenly said, "Dad?" in that way that tells you something important is about to happen.

"Yep!" I replied coolly.

"No, it's okay."

"What is it? You can ask anything." Both my councillors and the doctors had warned me about these moments.

"I dunno if I should ask…"

"But you already have."

"Ha! Yeah. You're so funny… sometimes!"

"Thanks! For the compliment."

"Seriously… I just wanted to know… what does it *feel like* to be… dying? Sorry, I mean how do you *feel*? It's just that you don't show any fear. Strachan says you might have got 'closure.' What does it mean? I looked it up, but it's just a word in a dictionary."

"Okay. That's a *few* questions and big ones too. I… I'm terrified, is the short answer. I could lie, but I don't want to do that with you. And no, I have no closure. If I had, I would feel at peace, but actually, I am… angry about it." Even *I* couldn't tell Jay *how* angry. He nodded slowly.

"Okay. That was it. Can we get ice-cream?"

"Sure. And thanks Jay."

"It's alright." He put his hand around my waist and I put my hand over around his shoulder. It was a rare moment of affection.

Day 180

I had a big argument with Christi this morning. I felt a lot of pain while getting out of bed. I almost gave up. It was 11.17 before I finally managed to pull my trousers on and shuffle out to the kitchen:

"Oh! *Arial*! I *thought* I heard you rummaging about!"

"Ha! Rummaging! I only wanted my trousers. What you heard was the sound of an *invalid*!"

"Well, at least you're up!"

"Yes. How about some breakfast."

"But you already had… Oh, I see. Extra rations for the War Hero!"

"Exactly. Especially after such a risky mission."

"Weetabix? Three?"

"With sugar, honey and nuts."

"Oh. Okay, the works." She busied herself preparing it. "There you go."

"Thanks." As I tucked into it, I watched the movement of her cute ass and lovely tit-mounds in minute detail.

"I've been thinking."

"Yes."

"Perhaps I haven't been as open with you as I should be."

"Really?"

"Christi. I am feeling terrible doubt. It's like nothing I have felt before. I feel as if all control has been taken away from me… no worse; I feel doubt that I *ever* had any control. I feel as if everything, *even you*, is an illusion."

Her back remained as silent as all backs do in these situations. Then she spoke.

"I've heard of that. I think I've read of it somewhere. Isn't it what teenagers feel?"

"Thanks!"

"Listen, if you want to reconnect, that's the wrong way of going about it."

"Well what the fuck *is* the right *way*? And why the *hell* are we disconnected anyway. It wasn't *me* that disconnected!"

"You're accusing *me*?"

"No! No! Jesus *Christ*! I'm *not* accusing Jesus Christ! Now you have me swearing in a foreign religion!"

To that, we both broke into laughter. Christi came over and sat gently on my lap, which I had to swivel clumsily to hold her.

"Oh, A! You're so funny. I miss the jokes, the funny little things, you see."

"Yeah … I know … But in reality you just want me for my *body*!" Desperation calls for Woody Allen. She kissed me. Halleluja! "Let's take this into the bedroom," I suggested, cupping the nearest breast. She has ample breasts since giving birth to Jay. They fill my hands. I rubbed her nipple mound.

"Oh yeah! Am I supposed to carry you, then?" she asked.

"Yes."

"How about here. You can take them out *here*."

I struggled with her bra-hooks for nearly a minute before she reached behind her and unfastened them for me. It's an age-old gesture of women that still excites me. I felt the beginning of an erection. I needed another joke, but I couldn't find it.

"Don't worry baby," she cooed. "There's always tonight."

"Yes, we will always have tonight!" I said in a Humphrey Bogart voice. But the joke came a few seconds too late. She climbed off my lap and flounced out of the room.

Shit! Failed. And how pathetic that I…

I'm in a desert. I crawl to an oasis and a giant, blue snake is barring my way to the water.

"You must hollow me if you want to live," he hisses.

"Hollow you? Don't you mean follow?"

But he has disappeared into a hole in the ground. I

crawl after him and catch up, inside a large, round chamber. An egg the size of a car is sitting on a log fire, in the centre of the chamber. The top suddenly lifts up and Adolf Hitler emerges on the end of a coiled spring. He does a little dance, with his legs dangling free, singing the Star Spangled Banner.

"Quick! In here!" hisses the snake, disappearing into the egg.

I climb in and see a tunnel. It's the snake's tail. I have to force myself inside it. Like a kid in a huge sock, I burrow my way up the snake's body, until my head emerges from its mouth. I shout with joy …

"Arial! Arial! Lie still! You passed out! I found you on the floor and I've called an ambulance!"

I opened my eyes. It was true enough. I lay on the floor; I could see the doorway from the viewpoint of a mouse. The floor looked even cleaner from this angle. I marvelled at the sheen my wife had given it.

Minutes later, a monumental paramedic called Olly peered down at me.

"Can you move your toes Mister Schechter? Let me see you move your toes."

I obliged him. He quickly established that my back wasn't broken, so they loaded me into an ambulance. We had to wait while Christi locked the house. She sat beside me and the ambulance wailed its way through suburbia. I twiddled my wife's index finger. For just an instant I felt her finger move to touch mine. It was enough for me.

Day 188

Well, that WAS an interesting week. The last entries were written on an old typewriter I bought, but I am back to writing in long-hand. I have been released from hospital where they had me under observation for three days, and THAT was only after the details were finally worked out for my private healthcare fund to be topped up from the re-mortgaging of my parents' house, God love 'em. But I'm unable to sit upright, so using the typewriter is out. I have to write this lying on my side.

Excuse me if it seems like I'm shouting, but as I explained, I can't do italics writing on my notepad.

At last Christi is paying attention to me and really talking to me.

Day 210

The going's good, apart from the bad dreams, which I now treat as reality. Since the incident in the kitchen, I have been on an increasing daily dose of pain-killers. Eventually this will be delivered by drip; a derivative of heroin, I'm told. It's funny; at last I will get to be a true hedonist. I should have done this years ago lol. See, I am resorting to texting language now.

Anyway, what I want to say is that reality and dreams are so blurred together now that I don't even try and differentiate. And the line, if there ever was one, is going to get even more blurred. I am entering that hazy world of medicated death.

I have seen more of the other lives I may have lived. I say 'may,' because they may instead be lives I dreamed in other, *real* lives. Who can tell? I saw an old monk praying at a pew, a pilot(?) of a spaceship so vast you could call it home, and some kind of medieval lord with his lover (who I may say was very attractive. If I lived with her, I wouldn't mind living THAT one again!). All these visions feel so real that I could touch the people in them. They are like memories, but I can't yet fill in the blanks.

I also keep remembering those damned steps. They go on forever, in some tomb-like shaft that seems to reach toward the centre of Earth. I am always creeping upward, on my hands and knees. I never seem to reach anything, not a door or a living thing.

Last night, for the first time, I saw a snatch of 'memory' about myself as an Irish, Catholic priest in some very early period. I can tell you that Rabbi Otis would not be happy; so far I don't appear to have been Jewish in ANY of my previous, or future, lives. I talked to Christi about it this morning.

"Here you go!" She announced the arrival of my late breakfast, carried in by her own beautiful hands, gripping the tray decorated with a painting of Runnymede that her father chose in a second-hand shop.

"Hey, darling. Can you just pull me up?" She did so after putting the tray on the bedside table, now reserved for the purpose. The clock had been removed. "Announcing the late Jimi Breakfast; eggs, bacon and fried bread. They don't make stars like that anymore!"

"Ha! Anything else you notice today?"

"Hm. Let me think." I had seen more of her breast that usual, down her low-cut t-shirt, when she lifted me. I was about to mention it when I noticed that her hair had been cut.

Phew! Close thing!

"Your hair!" A smile coursed across her face from cheek to cheek. "It looks great! For me?" She nodded. "I love you!"

She blushed, but didn't reply. I often told her I loved her. She often reciprocated, but not always. She bent over again to feed me. I confirmed to myself that she was showing more cleavage than usual.

"You're not wearing a bra?"

"After. Eat."

So I ate that breakfast as if it were my last, excuse the pun. I gobbled down the eggs, bacon and fried bread, and gulped down the coffee so fast we both giggled. I cheated though; the painkillers let me gulp down the coffee, even thought it burned my throat.

"You don't have to scrape the plate clean today," I suggested.

"Oh, but I do. You want to be a good boy, don't you?"

"Oh yes!"

"There! Finished. I guess an after dinner breast might

help to put you to sleep. Doctor's orders." She put aside the tray and pulled up her shirt to expose her breasts. Inadvertently, she left one nipple covered.

"Both."

"Oh, sorry."

I sucked gratefully on each nipple as she lowered it into my mouth. I wasn't grateful to her, you understand, but to God, for giving me this great woman. Her breasts were still as fantastic as ever; firm, full and quite round. Her nipples were a little worn, but I could only blame Jay's early teeth for this. I felt as if floated on a flying carpet and wasn't going to let the spell end.

"Um Um" I said persuasively.

"More? You are *greedy*. But you *have* been a good boy. Take your fill."

I sucked and sucked until the taste changed. I tried to lift my hand to grasp one of these beautiful faucets, but I failed. I lay back on the pillow, slightly out of breath. The breasts were recovered.

"I need you."

"I know, baby. You have me," she cooed.

"You know, one good thing has come out of all this…"

"What?"

"Well, I have seen lots of my previous lives now and NONE of them are Jewish. I seem to be more Catholic than Jewish. That should make a gentile happy!"

"Not this gentile … ."

"Gentile. Gentile, she said she was gentile. But I said; darling I want it ROUGH! Ha! Couldn't resist that old gem."

"It's good to hear you joke."

"Yeah, well … stand-up comedy always was my forte … ." I replied, quickly adding another joke. "Until I was bedridden."

"Ha! I have to go to your mother's. There's some paperwork, and then I am teaching this afternoon. Will you be okay?"

"Yeah. I'll be fine."

She left, and I WAS fine. I felt almost good. The drugs had almost drowned completely my fear of death. Only that dark, obdurate seed of doubt that still grew in the back of my mind, in a dark room where nobody goes, spread its black branches and bore its obsidian fruit of pain. I began to hope I would attain a drug-induced fog, whereby I could forget the pain of doubt.

Day 221

My new councillor, Dr Shally, has begun visiting me at home. I'm worried about him; the name Shally makes me think of comic-book pirates saying things like, "Shall 'ee do this or shall 'ee do that?" I wonder if the NHS hasn't assigned me the wackiest quack on their books, the guy that no one else will take. I thought about looking for a private councillor, but the cost of the private health care is already crippling my parents. By the way, they wanted me to move in with them, but I told them I don't need a series of lectures as my last contact with Earth. I think that quite upset them, but we have never seen quite eye to eye since I became a successful painter; I think they resented not being able to tell me, 'I told you so.' Dr Shally was here this afternoon:

"Well now Mr Schechter… can I call you Arial?"

"Why not. You are probably going to have to see me using a bedpan before this is over. You don't get much more intimate than that."

"Exactly. You can call me David."

"I think I will stick with Doctor Shally."

"As you wish. And may I say I have seen it *all* before. Now, the notes given to me by Pauline suggest you believe your dreams to be some kind of alternative reality. Would you like to tell me more about this?"

"Er. Well Pauline should have given you enough detail. You at least know about the tablets?"

"No. Pauline didn't give any details."

"Oh my God! It's like the most important thing to me now and she didn't even take notes!"

"Well, why don't you tell me all about it?"

I started to tell him about my dreams as coherently as possible, but I sounded like a lunatic. So I told him about my dream last night instead:

"Okay this was the latest dream. It's quite shocking. I am some kind of medieval lord in my castle and I guess I am pretty young; fourteen. I am in this toilet, or whatever they call them, with stone basins and taking a pee. This girl I grew up with, who I might say looks something like a young Kate Winslett or that blonde girl in Species, is sitting on the other … bowl. Anyway, I dunno how to say this politely … she reaches out and holds my cock while I am peeing. And I enjoy it! Let me say I would never do anything like this in … life … . And then she lifts her dress and I watch her PEE! It's a bit weird but I tell you, it's SO real!"

"I see. Interesting dream. Did you have such a friend?"

"Yes. But much later."

"It's interesting that you have trouble with the word 'dream.' And even more interesting that you use the word 'life' on its own without the word 'real.'"

"No I didn't."

"You did, actually. You said you would never, 'do anything like this in… life.'"

"Oh. Yes, I think I did. Well, that's because I'm no longer sure which IS reality."

"What else makes you think that?"

"These steps."

"Steps?"

"I'm climbing them, forever."

"I see."

"Yeah. But I *can't*. It's pitch black and there is no end to them. It's a kind of hell."

"But you said that sometimes you feel safe with this Satan character…?"

"Yeah. Sometimes. But I think it's a trick."

"And yet you believe the whole dream world, or worlds, that you… INHABIT. Couldn't they also be illusions? Couldn't he be tricking you?"

"Only if you believe in the Devil. Do you?"

"Well, I'm no theologian, but many men DO. I guess I DO, yes. Why can't *I* be Satan? Suppose you are dreaming NOW? Why don't you believe THAT?"

'Oh yeah! This is more like it! I like this game,' I thought. (I can't put this in caps 'cause it will confuse, so doing it like writers do thoughts.)

"Well, for one thing," I said. "You don't make me feel incredible doubt; doubt like I am not sure whether I have ever had any control or not."

"Hm. Doubt… Arial, is very common in people who are approaching the end of life."

"DYING! But I don't feel THAT sort of doubt…"

"Doubt about faith, I mean…"

"Yeah, and I'm telling you I don't feel any doubt about my faith. I am just as much a hopeful atheist as I EVER was. It's not THAT sort of doubt. It's doubt about my existence; whether this is real or not, whether I am ALIVE or not!"

"Oh Mr Schechter… You are definitely, very ALIVE! Well I don't want to tire you, so I think that's enough for today. It's given me a lot to think about and, I hope, you too. I will come back next week and we will explore this theme a bit more."

He stood up, packed a wad of notes into a brown leather briefcase and left.

"SHIT!" I said to the bare, white suburban walls of our bedroom.

Day 223

"What was that darling?" Christi said when Doctor Shally left. I had just been thinking that I should be nicer to him, because at least he tried to understand what I said, but then I started coughing. A spray of orange blood spattered the white and purple design on the duvet. I couldn't answer Christi, but she could hear me coughing. She ran into the room and lifted my neck to clear my airway. The coughing soon subsided, but we both stared at the blood stain in horror.

"Well, this is it!" I whispered.

"Don't talk like that."

I looked at her. She looked away. I felt shocked. It wasn't what I had been expecting from the new, warm and caring Christi. And today I had another shock.

Just about the last thing I can do for myself is surf the internet using our old Dell laptop. I can still explore the world with my index finger. I wanted to research mental health and Devil, so I went to put that phrase into google and it auto-completed to show 'Mental health and death.'

'Must be something Christi was searching for,' I thought. I let that be my search phrase and looked at the results. One of them, 'Advice for Carers,' had been clicked on, so I followed that. The section 'Advice for Wives' caught my eye. It read, 'If both of you have been used to breast-play during your married life, let your husband play with your breasts, at least once each week. This will relieve the boredom and stress and maintain a healthy bond between you both.'

I felt such a mentsh. Here was I, thinking she had found a way to love me again and she had just been following instructions from some damned website. I knew then that we hadn't really connected AT ALL.

By the way, I am going to try and describe as much as I can about my OTHER lives, as a sort of living testament. If it's any use to anybody else, then great!

Anyway, I have made a resolution. If I am going to win back Christi, it will only be possible using one method; humour. I have an idea. I found out the other day that she is secretly reading my notes.

***

I am going to let my Woody Allen out and hope that
she reads it and falls back in love with me again. I am
tearing out this page and hiding it. I will leave a note
about it in my Will. Which reminds me, I haven't written
my one yet! Ha! Ha!

Day 225
The pain, when it burst through, usually when
somebody forgets to refill my drip, is indescribable. Most
of the time I float around in a strange fog of half-dreams,
half-reality.

This evening Jay came to sit with me. He had seen an
article in The Telegraph (that boy really is growing too
fast!) about the Retrospective of my work being presented
at the Wolfrestson Gallery, in Gower Street. I knew about
it of course, but had forgotten. It makes me laugh that it's
a retrospective. I'm not even dead yet! I might have been
suspicious that my agent, Dorothy, is just trying make a
bit more money – she did ask me for any new work to put
in the show – but I know her too well. She is more likely
trying to motivate me to keep working. I did try and put
brush to canvas last week, with Christi's help, but all I
managed was one bold, red, stroke and one short,
ominous, black one. I guess if I were a Picasso or Dali,
one might get something for it. It's under the bed now.

Anyway, my mind wanders. Yes, Jay told me about the
show and spent nearly an hour with me. He looked
frightened; I could see it in the corners of his eyes. But
it's what's in the corners of his mind that frightens ME. I
don't know what to say to him, however. I tried to keep it
light, but I could see he wanted to ask if I am still
frightened.

"Yes Jay, I am frightened, but not so much as I was," I
told him. "I keep seeing these other lives Jay. I really do
believe now in reincarnation. I don't know where I am
going next, but I am sure it's somewhere."

He nodded slowly, but kept his eyes on me. I think he

felt satisfied. If he was, it was my best bit of lying yet; I should get a job as a funeral's salesman; "Get your coffins here! Guaranteed eternal life in Heaven with the Rosebud Mark I coffin!" Ha! Damn! Shouldn't have said that, should I? But I am allowed a little bit of fear every now and again, aren't I?

My mind rambles so much now. The truth is that I'm not reassured by the thought of more lives, not if I am just the play thing of the Devil. I want to escape the feeling that I don't have a will, a reality of my own. It occurred to me today that I might be imagining my own death. Perhaps, in some perverse way, I am willing it. Perhaps the tablets never existed. I wonder if it's too late to try believing in my NOT DYING?

***

The Steps

Well, the Ariel story was hardly written using good grammar, but you could say it was impressionistic, the sort of thing a painter would write, if he *could* write. I am beginning to believe these books record my lives, as He tells me.

I almost feel like throwing myself off these steps! Just for the jolly hell of it! It would relieve the boredom. It is funny, I am starting to remember fragments of lives besides the one that ended in the trenches, but none of them seem real. That is, they seem real, but I don't remember their outcome. They are in the past and seem like memories, but I never know what will happen next, or what came before. In that sense it is like looking into the life of another person. Actually, I have a sneaking suspicion that some of the lives are not *remembered*, but in the future, like the one about the ore-carrier. It is so big that you could fly around inside it with one of today's Royal Observer Corp's aeroplane.

Perhaps I am some kind of shaman, these dreams being visions that I have while sleeping? I find that reassuring, but then there are these damned steps. Why would any shaman worth his salt spend an eternity climbing stone steps?

I just thought I heard a sound! A sound in here, other than Satan's voice, would be a world-changing, a life-changing experience. But afterwards, I realised there had *been* no echo. In here there certainly *would* be. I have never known an emptier place. When I use any words like 'never,' or anything to do with time, it is cause to pause. Time seems almost irrelevant here. Perhaps there really is no time? I have heard some lunatic scientists speculating such.

What crazy kind of existence *is* it in here! It's

infuriating, frustrating and soul-destroying! Ha! I have never eaten a morsel, or drank a drop of water since I came here. It can't be the same day, or even set of a few days. I have decided to start counting the steps as I climb. That way I might be able to estimate how long I have been here, or how long I spend climbing. Today I just reached one thousand, four hundred and twenty-four.

It seems to me that the fetid odour wafting up the stairwell is a little less strong. But I could be wrong.

***

Despair! Despair! I know an utter despair beyond all that I had imagined possible. If it had not been sudden, it would be impossible for a human soul to reach it.

I had been crawling up these sodding infinite, bloody, stone steps as usual. As usual, I didn't know whether it was night or day, past or future, so to speak, in relation to any of the lives or events in my mixed up, tangled memory. My fingers lighted on something in the step, a defect. I felt it carefully. It felt like a notch! Yes, it most certainly is a notch. I just checked it because I am still sitting next to it. I remember carving just such a notch shortly after remembering, or living, a life as David MacIntyre. Do you remember? The terrible thing is that I'm not sure if it is a notch that *I* carved. The only way I am going to find out is by climbing for what I guess to be a day and then looking for another notch. But since the concept of 'day' has no meaning in here, that is a senseless strategy. Moreover, I might find another notch, which turns out to be this one, the very same notch! I cannot stand it anymore! I am going insane! These steps might just be endless. I might just be a mouse on an insane treadmill, like Escher's impossible staircase. There is no beginning or end to this Hell!

***

I have searched my mind, my memory, ceaselessly,

looked under every thought, every fear, every emotion, for signs that would lead me to knowledge of my first life, my real life. At last, I have something. I will call her Byblis, since I can no longer remember her name.

I cannot clearly see our house, although I remember a fierce yellow sunlight piercing my eyes when I awoke on my parents' bed. They were not there. The house lay empty. I turned over and surprised away the entwining, chubby arms of Byblis, who had lain behind me.

I no longer know how it began, perhaps we talked of our dreams, of castles and faeries, but I found myself, resplendent in that wild energy only pre-school children must expend, so I climbed atop the vast, oak wardrobe, after first scaling its sibling chest of drawers. I peered comically at my upside-down image in the mirror on the wardrobe's door and stood up to spread my arms in victory.

I looked down on Byblis, spread-eagled on the bed, and suddenly launched myself into death-defying space. Miracle child-moments seemed to pass in the air before I landed, with my legs straddling her.

"I am a dragon and I have come to eat you!" I roared.

Of course, she squealed with a mixture of delight and mock-fear, as any budding actress-maiden would, and I climbed and jumped again.

Each time I jumped, the wide-eyed horror in her eyes became more real and gave me the tiniest erection, the first I can remember. There seemed nothing as appropriate as undressing her.

"Are you going to eat me?" she pleaded, without resisting.

"Yes."

I peeled back her pink cloth until she lay as if ravaged, but smiling. I licked and I licked before kissing her every inch. But my body had outsped my knowledge of what to do next and the passion subsided.

Her eyes shone for me evermore.

And now all I have is this dreadful corridor, this collection of steps with no purpose!

"If there is anybody in here, trapping me, you have to speak to me now, now, now!"

"I cannot stand this anymore… more… more"

"Hey you! Are you here, here, here? Who are you, you, you? What do you want, want, want? Are you God, God, God? Or the Devil … ? Devil … ? Devil? Hey … ! Hey … ! Hey … ! Speak to me … ! me … ! me … ! Answer me … ! me … ! me … !"

"Am I alive … ? alive … ? alive … ? Or dead … ? dead … ? dead … ?"

***

I have been sitting in the steps, thinking, for hours. I have had some kind of epiphany, perhaps brought on by total despair, who knows?

Satan, if it is he, told me that; doubt was his 'gift' to me, the only thing I could be certain of. But he is *wrong*! As Descartes says; I know I exist because I think. I *remember* my first existence on these steps and even *then*, I *knew* I existed. Satan is lying. I feel a sense of triumph, because I have outwitted Him! He doesn't completely control me! It gives me just the slenderest ray of hope.

***

I don't know if it has anything to do with my epiphany, but I found something! I climbed the steps and came to the usual landing, but then I hit a wall! I have reached the top of the steps! What is more, I can feel two vertical cracks in the wall opposite, through which a draft whispers. A door! I have tried pushing it, gripping the edge and finding some kind of handle but so far, nothing. What to do?

***

I'm not sure if it happened, or it was another dream

while I slept, but again I found myself in the chair, making that terrible choice with the tablets.

This time, however, I refused to choose.

"I know your game now," I told him. "You are a liar and have no power over me anymore. You give me life, only to take it away. I don't know what perverted pleasure you gain from this. You only know about torture, about inflicting pain. You didn't have a father or mother, so you know *nothing* of love! Only fear and pain."

"I do know love. My Father loves me. And why do you tell me this? What new knowledge do you think you have?"

"You told me I could only know doubt. But I know that I exist!"

"Yes. That is true. I told you I have a problem with speaking ambiguously. Nevertheless, in here, you can only know doubt. Until you choose. Choose!"

"No! Tell me now; am I alive or dead? Is this Heaven or Hell?"

"Choose! I command you. Or I shall leave you here!"

For the first time, the friendly smile had left my tormentors face. He turned and passed behind my left shoulder. As He passed, I saw, for the first time, His feet emerge from beneath his long, velvet coat. They were hideous; misshapen hooves with toes like a bird's talons. Between those He walked on, He dragged a third, vestigial hoof. I tried to turn, but seemed pinned to the chair. I heard a door shut and I felt myself released. I stood and ran to the wall behind me. I could see the outline of a door, which He must have passed through, but there seemed to be no handle. I listened at the crack and heard the scraping sound of His claws on the hard stone. Try as I might, I could not open the door. But then I found myself lying awake on a landing of these endless steps.

***

I sat as still as a statue, thinking. In fact, I didn't know how still I had become, so deep were my thoughts, until I heard a scraping sound on the other side of the 'door.' There could be no doubt what caused the sound; Satan's dragging hoof.

"Are you scared of me?" I bellowed.

But his steps only receded.

"You *are*! You're afraid of me! Come back!"

I pushed at the door in desperation. I pushed until my shoulder seemed on fire. In my deepest, darkest moment of despair, I pushed once more. The door creaked open.

I couldn't wait until it closed. So, gasping for air, I lurched through the door before collapsing on a stone floor. I lay there until I could sit, and finally stagger, to my feet.

Unused to seeing, I only gradually became aware of a pale, flickering light, in the distance. I blinked, rubbed my eyes and staggered toward it. I emerged onto the tiny landing of yet another set of steps, this time a spiral one.

"Oh no! Not more!"

My sudden surge of optimism died immediately. But I could hear a new noise, outside the walls and, accompanying it, a shaking of the stone around me. I listened closely and knew it to be the sound of crashing waves against the stone.

I had to choose whether to go up or down. Something drew me down. On impulse, I gingerly trod the stone steps, ever downward, the sound of my footfall accompanied by the increasing thunder of waves against the foundations of whatever building I occupied.

The yellow light came from tapers, bolted to the wall at periodic intervals. But as I descended the light became redder.

Eventually, I could hear water slapping against the steps inside the building. I took one last turn and met with the sight I had half-expected. Water covered the lowest steps and, as the storm outside raged, so the wavelets lapped against the stone steps. Below their bottle green surface, I saw that the steps continued on, who knew to what depth. I dare not go further, but sat on a step, considering the situation. My hands, visible before me for the first time, were bathed in a deep, red light and I laughed.

I laughed at the meaninglessness of the steps, of the meaninglessness of life. I felt despair, and laughed at it.

Shaking my head, I turned and ascended, past my original entrance point and on toward the top of the steps, if such a place existed.

Imagine my surprise, given the similarity of the tower to a lighthouse, when I actually emerged onto a platform, containing a giant, slowly rotating, glass lantern.

I had to stoop as the beam passed, to avoid being blinded.

"Welcome," said a familiar, smooth voice from somewhere. I continued around the lantern and saw the face or my tormentor once more. Now, I knew that the person in front of me was Satan. "Look outside," He told me. I did.

All around the lighthouse the sea seemed blood-red. Looking more closely, I saw a ghastly sight. Thousands, probably millions, of dead bodies, crashed into the stone tower with the force of the stormy waters. Clouds blackened the sky, obscuring the sun, if there was one.

"Where are we?" I asked

"At the end of your existence."

His reply sent a cold shiver down my spine.

"Look more closely at the bodies," He told me.

As I looked more closely, I began to discern the faces of the bodies and one that I recognised, that of a friend. As I looked, the faces grew more became recognizable until I knew that all the people I had cared for were crashing against the tower.

"What is the meaning?" I asked.

"You, see, even I can generate a strong light. It doesn't

need God. You think that God is 'light,' but not all light is his. I can give you life again. Will you choose?"

"No."

Satan seemed to laugh. A blackness came over me and I found myself back on the endless steps again. When I reached for the door I found only more steps.

I thought perhaps I might be spared furthermore that particular torture of the library, but He took me there again. In those dark hours before He came I had returned to considering faith and whether I could I ever have been a holy man. Now I put the idea to Him.

"Perhaps a holy man would be able to resist your tablets. Perhaps the most devout of monks could resist the temptations of female flesh."

He tossed me another book, entitled Monk.

***

Monk

At the eleventh hour of the day my duties in the dairy for the morning had been completed and I was, as usual, in contemplation. Kneeling in the third pew back of the main Abbey Chapel, I watched the glossed back of the black ant. Reflecting the pillar of holy light shafting through the stained-glass window, the tiny ant's carapace dipped up and down as it negotiated the uneven surface of the Bible rail. This has always been my favourite time of day.

But this day in particular, something felt different. Deep inside me, in the nebulous area where dreams of the night before are placated by the ambitions of the day ahead, something surprising lurked. Malignant and hard, like a vinegar-boiled conker, it just wouldn't be shifted. Not a memory, or an idea, however, it *was* more like a memory. This felt the more surprising, since my memory had never been good. Indeed, I could barely remember my childhood, but relied on others for its details.

With all that the teaching that the ancients, such as Aristotle, and our more modern thinkers, like Bernard of Clairveaux, had imparted to me, you would think I could rid myself of unwanted thoughts. But they swaggered through my mind like miscreants on a village street.

Suddenly, the full horror of the thought expanded in my mind into an image I could not contemplate or articulate. I shuddered, closed my eyes and prayed with all the devotion I had in me. Slowly, so very slowly, the thought subsided and shrank back into the depths of my soul.

We practised the Eight Offices, praying on the hour at eight set times of the day, as had been the custom of most monasteries for 600 years. After the sixth-hour, or Midday Prayer, I set myself to contemplation, as is required by my

Order.

Behind the Abbey Chapel, a shot greensward lay before an orchard, which led down an almost impassable precipice above the banks of the river. Beyond the great river white-tipped mountains ranked into the distance. An excellent place for further contemplation, I often visited the sward. Unlike the Cloisters on the south side of the Abbey, the orchard only had sun for a few hours each day. Fronting the orchard were two ancient cherry trees. They had long forborne the onerous task of bearing fruit and were now in dignified 'retirement.'

In the crisp light of autumn, one could easily tell the time from the line of shadow cast by their two trunks. I called the tree on the right Augustine and that on the left, Auguste. This day I felt not so much as a breeze, so after checking about me for any unwanted witness, I reached out and placed my hand on the bark of Auguste.

You won't be touched today by your admirer, my friend, so I will do it. I am sure The Virgin Mary will forgive me this beneficent gesture on Her behalf.

With the help of only a small breeze, Augustine's outermost branches, which had reached for their admirer's most days for many a long year, would gently touch her partner's like a caress. The faintest whisper of a breeze rose up from the valley and touched my cheek. Its invisible hands made the two trees' leaves rustled against each other with that sound that relaxed me. Tension, present since the morning's last contemplation, left and I felt ready to examine what dark form lurked within my thoughts. I walked over to the bench I had hewn with my own hands many years before, and sat down.

Yes, it was Satan who had visited me. I had not felt that awful presence for a long time. Of course, his temptations were ever-present, but not himself. I felt that he wanted to say something to me, but I could not be sure that listening would not be a sin.

Surely simply ignoring a danger rather than

understanding it, especially in this enlightened age, would still be considered a danger? Ah, but not in the case of Satan.

I would have to ask the Abbot. I breathed in the fresh air and strolled around the bench in uneasy contemplation, until the bell for the Seventh Hour rang. This day it was to be the hour for the meeting in the Chapter House, since the Abbot was not due to return to the Abbey until that hour. I made my way to the venerable house and took my seat in the semi-circle, all of us ordered according to age. I sat now, disconcertingly, only third from the end of the line.

The Abbot named the Saints for the day and then we prayed for departed monks. He then read a chapter from Saint Benedictine's Rule and commenced that task of giving us our duties for the day. He turned to me.

"Brother Arnaud. For you I have a special duty. I have a problem which has vexed me for some time. You will oversee the lay-brothers, building the Cloisters for the new annex for the sisters. They have not, as yet, an Abbess and, for now, will be reporting to me. However, I'm too busy to oversee the work myself and I am also not skilled in the working of wood and stone. I remembered that you had at least experience with wood in your previous life…"

"Yes. I am able to take on this task, if you ask it."

"Good. Good. I see that you understand the sensitivity of this work. Would you mind staying awhile to talk over the details after we finish here?"

I shook my head and smiled. The Abbot always approved economy of speech. He quickly dismissed the other monks.

"Walk with me in the garden," he began. "I can assume you understand the sensitivity of this work?"

"Of course."

"Within the Papal Enclosure there must be absolutely *no* impropriety. Sister Justyne is the most senior sister and therefore you will work closely with her. I use the word 'closely' with caution."

The Abbot seemed lost in contemplation for a moment, so I followed his movement around the garden, watching his leather-bound toes swishing the long grass every time they protruded from under his habit. He coughed once and continued:

"I did consider Brother Ranier and Brother Ansel for the work. Both are more senior than you, but both are ailing and neither have experience of wood-working. Furthermore, you have, over the many years I have known you, been a man of suitable self-discipline. Sister Justyne and I have discussed the work at length and I would like you to set up a system of working within the enclosure, whereby the lay-brothers are required as little as possible. As much construction should take place outside as possible and the half completed work assembled within. You may select, after a suitable period of, say, one week, three lay-brothers whom you most trust to do this work. Sister Justyne has suggested that the nuns will do much of the manual work themselves. I tried to argue her out of *this*, but she insisted. My reluctance came not from a consideration for the *physical* weakness of her sex, you understand, but rather the spiritual weakness that is the ferment of Satan…"

"I understand." Actually, I wasn't sure what the Abbot meant by 'ferment;' he often used words in unfamiliar ways to express his own subtle ideas on temptation, and this seemed another such use of a word to me. Of one thing I felt certain; I was, as the Abbot said, worthy of his trust in the matter of female temptation. I hadn't thought of women's physical forms for many years and had not had need to relieve the excessive seminal fluid for even longer. Mine had never been a difficult transition from the secular to the religious life.

"Do you think you are ready to take on this work? You can refuse, if you think it beyond you. I would like you to leave after Mid-Afternoon Prayer and return before Night Prayer."

"I am ready for the work Abbot. But I did not think the new monastery ground had been consecrated yet, so can we say that the Papal Enclosure actually exists?"

"Yes. I too have thought on this. However, since it is an annex of our own monastery the situation is not clear. Let us not take the risk. Our Order is still expanding fast and we cannot risk embarrassment in front of the Languedoc nobility. Pope Honorius would not like it!"

"No. That is certainly something to be avoided."

"Good. Good. One last thing. It has come to my attention that you too suffer from some ailment. That is, when emptying the garderobes, a brother has found red liquid after you have used the bucket."

I remained silent. It felt strange to be addressed so directly about something I had hidden for so long.

"Do you deny it?" he asked.

"I am aware of it Abbot. It does not prevent me from carrying out my duties and it gives me little discomfort… as yet."

"I have heard of such a thing before. It is very serious. You know that?"

"Yes."

"Very well. Report back to me tonight, before you go to your bed. Good luck."

With a dismissive flutter of his bejewelled hand, the Abbot left me. I hastened to my cell, to prepare myself for the task. After Mid-Afternoon Prayer I left, through the Monastery gate.

The road from the village lay thick with viscous mud, from the early autumn rains and the waggons that had been bringing up building materials for the last few days. A wide, high wall separated both monasteries, so I had to follow the track around to the new entrance under construction. Even this short distance caked my habit with brown mud.

"I am here to see Sister Justyne," I said to the first nun I saw. She nodded nervously and beckoned me onto the clean grass, inside the gate. There I waited, not quite sure what else to do.

I hadn't met Sister Justyne before. I only knew that she came from the lowlands. When she lifted her face, so that the shadow of her habit was removed from her features, I saw intense, brown eyes and a warm smile. She stood tall, not much shorter than myself, and had a steady, calming voice, not deep but certainly melodious. She looked slightly younger than I, but still an old woman. I felt no physical attraction to her, so I thought that the Abbot's fears were unfounded.

"Come with me Brother Arnaud," she said quietly. "It's very good to have you with us. The work has been getting a little beyond my skill during the last few days."

She led me to the site of the future Cloisters, where the foundations were already laid in heavy, white stone. Thick, squared-off, oak uprights had been inserted into the post holes and began to show the skeleton of the future building. Several lay-brothers put down their tools and nodded, half-bowing to me, when I passed. One stole a quick glance at the receding back of the Sister.

The head-builder had laid out the Cloister plans on a table and stood silently by while the Sister and I perused them.

"It looks sturdy enough." I asked the man. "What is your schedule?"

"We hope to have all the verticals in place before the end of the month Brother Arnaud"

"You don't recognise me. Do you remember little Mattheu, who threw an apple at your back and missed, many years ago? You punished me properly, in front of my friends, as I remember!" His face reddened.

"Ah yes! I remember you… and your father. A good man. Is he still with us?"

"Long gone Brother."

"Well, you can forget feeling guilty about the apple. It's a very long time ago and I behaved far worse as a child. You will one day teach me a thing or two. In fact, you can start now." His face brightened.

"Yes Monsieur! I mean; Brother!"

"What are these on the plan? Do you have enough wood to complete the work for this month, if you include these?"

A crack of thunder announced the afternoon rain that usually arrived at this time. I felt miserable, working in such muddy, damp conditions, but such would be the routine for the next three weeks. I reported back to the Abbot on time that evening and took to my straw bed, feeling weary but content.

Within a week the horizontal stonework courses were being laid and I could order heavy linen sheets to be stretched across the top of the vertical posts to create a shelter. I noticed the men often steal disapproving glances at the Sister and, for her part, she spoke curtly, or even rudely, to the men and she seemed just as ill-tempered with her own flock of sisters, although she was very polite to me.

"We have this!" announced Sister Justyne, carrying something wrapped in cloth at the beginning of the second month. She lifted up the hem of cloth to reveal the tip of a gold cross. "It has been donated by one of the other monasteries." To my quizzical expression she replied, "They have purchased a new one."

"Very good. The Abbot tells me this *is* consecrated ground. And even if it is not, I often pray in my own cell. Do you?"

"Oh yes. Very often. We can pray together, just before you leave every evening."

I felt somewhat surprised at the suggestion, so raised my eyebrows.

She continued, "We can pray for the successful conclusion of our building work!"

"Yes."

I ordered Mattheu and his men to build us a makeshift pew and Bible at the eastern end of the covered Cloister and we used an overturned box as a temporary altar. During the fourth week of construction an event occurred that would mark a turning point in my life, dwindling though it had been. Because the men had not much spare material to construct the pew, they had made it short. Consequently, the two of us had to sit and kneel close together. Thus I could hear each one of her gentle breaths while we prayed.

During one particularly melancholy evening, with heavy rain pattering on the wet linen roof, I thought I heard Sister Justyne weeping. I continued to pray, but part of me couldn't help listening and then I knew it. She *was* weeping. This seemed the more surprising, since I had come to think of her as a stern woman in her daily routine. Now I had the almost irresistible urge to glance at her. It would, however, be impossible for me to comfort her, because our vows did not permit such interactions between a monk and nun, unless it were in confession. This weeping reoccurred several times during prayer over the next few days, until I could stand it no longer. We were always alone during prayer. The Lay Brothers were not permitted to pray at the same time as we, so I suddenly turned to her:

"What is ailing you Sister?" I must have sounded angry and I regretted this.

"It is nothing Brother. I am old and infirm. I am prone to various pains and ills. I… I… No, it doesn't matter."

Her reply irritated me more than if she had kept silent. Now she had raised many questions in my mind, which I tried to dismiss, but they persisted and began to have a life of their own. Soon, I found myself developing tender feelings toward the Sister, feelings which would be confirmed to my conscious mind during an encounter she had with one of the other Sisters.

"What are you doing Sister Agnes?" she admonished. "That bucket is too full! You are spilling half of it. If it is too heavy for you to carry, get one of the other sisters to help you, or lighten the load!"

"Yes Sister Justyne!"

Though the girl looked hurt by the rebuke, I felt angry with *her*, not Sister Justyne.

'This is not good!' I told myself. I began to think about talking to the Abbot about my feelings.

That evening Sister Justyne and I both prayed as usual. I had begun reciting the Lord's Prayer, which I usually did first, when I thought I felt something touch my hand. I thought it might be a fly, so attempted to flick it off but felt something bigger. I finished the prayer with some difficulty and glanced to my left. Sister Justyne's hand lay against mine and she had started to weep again. I felt my member, that most forgotten of limbs, harden, something that shocked me. I hadn't felt this for so long that I believed it would never happen again.

"What are you doing?" I muttered

"We are old," she whispered.

I sometimes wonder how it is women managed to make pithy remarks which nevertheless, somehow, seem self-evident. If law courts made decisions purely based on verbal delivery, women would make the best lawyers. I could not, for the life of me, think of a suitable response. I could only nod and look into her brown eyes. She held my gaze and, for a moment, I believed that what she did was not wrong. The effect of this thought acted like a stone entering a pool. The ripples spread through my soul until the calm water resembled a living, boiling body of water. I finished praying and somewhat abruptly, left for the security of my cell. I prayed through the night for my own soul. I did not, however, mention it to any of the brothers, or confess.

The following day Justyne – now, save my soul, I though of her has simply Justyne – grew bolder. I had hardly begun to pray when she took hold of my hand. Her's felt cool to the touch and so delicate that I experienced a welling of emotion. I clasped her own hand between my own and continued to pray, but for both of us and I admit that I gave her little hand a tiny squeeze before finally releasing it. Now I had become an accomplice. There could be no going back. I didn't even pray for our souls that night, and went to work the following day almost sanguine about our secret alliance.

When one is dying melancholy replaces the light of day, and a yawning chasm of doubt, the dark of the blackest night hours. I had felt this, every day and night. But despite my devout prayers to protect me, a strange light had come into the darkness of night and set the sun again upon the heavens, if only for a while. So I knelt to pray that evening, in the expectation that her fingers would light on my hand. But something had started to move my habit.

She is just moving closer to me. Why not? We are two souls joined in our quest. Quest?

My habit lifted, something cool grasp my hard member and she murmured something, but it did not sound like any prayer I knew. I found it impossible to pray myself, so murmured gibberish and reached under her habit without thinking. Her genitals, when my fingers found them, were warm and slightly moist, but I felt an impulse to glance at her. She may have seen fear in mine, but her eyes calmed me with their approval, so I inserted one finger into her and held it there while she held on to my member.

"I will wear less next time," she whispered, when we walked to the linen door-flap.

***

I lay awake that night in terror for my soul, but neither Satan nor God visited me. In the morning I saw that a gentle breeze encouraged Augustine's touch of Auguste with her leafy limbs. I smiled and, catching myself smile, looked up to Heaven.

"Did I do wrong God?"

I heard no sound but the 'creak' as Auguste's upper limbs rubbed against his admirer's. The vortex of wind that had moved him came down to Earth and whipped the hem of my habit. I could be wrong, but I felt it to be a sign, a sign that, in the Sight of God, somehow I had not sinned, or that my Sin grew less than my Beneficence, such as a meek monk can bestow.

Due to inclement weather, a construction hiatus of four days occurred. I spent much time in my cell, sometimes peering out of my slot at the blurred autumn landscape, but most often reading passages from the Bible and works of Saint Bernard. I looked for something that might condone my liaison with Sister Justyne. I had tried to explain it to myself as some new form of religious expression; that the Sister and I were in some kind of Divine ecstasy, but in my heart I knew that I had fallen in love. I had experienced love as a teenager:

Mine felt like an almost inevitable entrance into the Holy Order. When aged four, my mother had died while giving birth to my baby sister. Her death left my father to care for three boys and a baby alone, a daunting task, but he had work as a carpenter to the local Chevalier. He succeeded in placing my eldest brother as a squire to the Chevalier and decided that the second eldest would inherit the business. My father had little capital, so had often told me, youngest of the three, of his intention to sell me to the local monastery. Always a solitary boy, I spent much of my time in contemplation anyway. I didn't much care for girls yet, so when he told me that year that he had struck a deal with the Cistercian Abbot, it was with equanimity that I accepted my fate. In return for me he received four silver denier, a considerable sum and more than I would have been worth, were I not skilled with wood. Thus I became a carpenter and moved from monastery to monastery, until I ended up at one of the greatest.

There, aged twelve I met Edmee. Blonde and fresh as an Alpine flower, I later learned that she was the daughter of a local cowherd, but, to me, she was a princess. After much bashful wooing I managed to kiss her, but one of the brothers saw me, which precipitated the end of my tenure at that monastery and resulted in my journey here.

A day came when the storm had finally abated. I had noticed some pain, during the night, on both sides of my hips, but when I rose from my bed, it became so intense, I had to sit down. Eventually, I found I could stand with some difficulty, so I went about my morning duties. Upon leaving the Seminary, I saw the Abbot walking along the Cloisters with his hands behind his back,. The alternate shafts of light and shadows cast stripes across his hunched profile. I felt something like affection for him and followed, almost stepping on the hem of his habit when he suddenly stopped and turned. I looked into his grey eyes and saw my chance to confess, but I concealed my thoughts and smiled. My moment of salvation had passed.

As I left to meet Justyne I wondered if our love might be God's reward for the pain of my suffering. Perhaps *she* would be my reward. Justyne maintains that it is part of a journey that God wishes us to make, part of His strange plan for us. But the uncomfortable idea that it might be Temptation made itself known to me.

Justyne smiled at me as usual when I arrived. She had treated both her sisters and the lay-brothers harshly as usual, so they left early, leaving us alone to pray.

"Why do you treat them so? Without patience?" I enquired.

"I do not know. Perhaps because I am impatient to be with… you. Every time I say a harsh thing I repent. My nights are long and cold. I will endeavour to be more patient Brother. Will you not teach me patience?"

"You must learn from the Good Book. I cannot instruct. You forget, I am not ordained."

"But your hand…? It's the hand of God's will."

"Is it? I thought it was the hand of… of… your will and mine."

"No. Say not so."

"Let us try to pray."

"Very well."

I knelt and pulled her down beside me. She seemed as reluctant as a frightened sheep. While I prayed, I heard the gentle rustle of her habit. I thought perhaps she felt agitated, so I continued to pray, but when I opened my eyes, I saw that she had stripped to the waist. I could not recall my mother's breasts and had only seen crude representations before. Justyne's were not firm, but not yet as unsightly as some old hag that inhabited the chatter of the monks. My member hardened more than before.

"What are you doing?" I whispered.

"I feel cleaner like this. Don't you approve? Show me with your hand that what we do is not a sin."

I felt angry with her for a moment, angry at the insidious pretention of her argument, but I reached out and cupped one of her breasts, noticing that it still felt quite firm to the touch. I slid my hand down over the flat belly and thought that she must once have been a beautiful woman.

"I have so long wanted the touch of a man… a man with a clean spirit."

Her nubs were hard. I felt moved almost to ecstatic tears. I stood and so did she, so that we faced each other. I held her shoulders, half intending to admonish her, half to caress her. I wanted to kiss her very much, but I had only kissed a girl once and the pain of that memory made me flinch.

"I have never been kissed," she said, as if reading my thoughts.

I leaned toward her soft, flesh-pink lips and placed my

own against them. It was as if two, dry autumn leaves rustled against eachother. But when her saliva moistened the bond, we kissed passionately. Only then did I notice how tightly I had been holding her shoulders, the shape of my hands leaving white imprints on those lovely limbs. She quickly pulled up her habit, replaced her scapular and let me by the hand to the new oak door.

***

The Cloister had been completed before the end of Winter and the Abbot, pleased with my work, instructed me to commence work on a small chapel, to the northern side of the Cloister.

All the lay-brothers and sisters worked well as a team, so that the foundations were soon laid. The Chapel would have a small tower. Within this would be a tight, winding staircase, leading first to a tiny gallery for musicians, and beyond, to the bell-tower. Ours would be of small, but ambitious design. The lower floor was to have a stone encasement, but wood above that, except for the tower itself, whereof it was feared the bells' vibration might shake a wooden structure to pieces.

Justyne and I met the spring like two children in a Grecian paradise. My childhood had been snatched away from me too early and, like her, I revelled in our explorations. We both knew next to nothing about sexual intercourse, so each new step brought great joy and many half-guilty Hail Mary's, but knew how lucky were were to explore each other in the Cloister, whose concealed sanctuary none of the lay-brothers or sisters would dare violate the strict prohibition on entering during our prayers.

As work commenced on the Chapel floor and first courses of stone wall, I began to wonder what it would be like to be inside Justyne. Until now, we had brought each other to innocent ecstasies by means of our hands alone. I was considerably surprised, even shocked, when during the first week of June, J, as I now called her when short of breath, placed her delicate lips around my member and gently licked its blushing end. I felt overcome with shame, but acquiesced to what I believed was God's cause, and laid back to enjoy the sensation. She proceeded to lick and caress my member with the tip of her tongue, until I could bear it no longer and released my sexual humor in one shuddering column of ecstasy.

Neither of us believed for one moment that we were completely devoid of shame. At our greatest heights of ecstasy, we felt that in some way we were doing God's work, but not in the sense that sexual gratification was *itself* the goal. No, we felt that God wanted to lead us through a vale of the Devil's temptation to some paradise beyond. What this might be, neither of us could quite see, but we were eager to be God's instrument in reaching this Promised Land.

I overheard the lay-brothers talking about sexual union near the well. I hid myself behind a tree and absorbed as much of their conversation as I could. Later, I would consult the Scriptorium's stock of manuscripts to decipher the words' meaning. I did so, but one word had escaped the writers of these colourful manuscripts; the word 'cock.' I had to trick one of the lay-brothers into telling me its meaning:

"Brother Henri?" I asked him. "I heard you and other brothers discussing the word 'cock' yesterday. What does this word normally mean Brother?" He blushed deeply.

"Sorry Brother. I didn't mean…"

"Just answer the question."

"A foul, Brother; a bird that eats grain and makes the hens lay eggs."

"Good. And what is the other meaning of the word?"

The bashful brother took a moment to reply.

"Our male member Brother. The thing that goes hard when we see a pretty girl. Don't ask me to…"

"That's enough. Now we don't allow that sort of

language, or those *thoughts*, in the Monastery. You should remember that, if you want to continue here. Now go about your work and pass on my message to the other brothers."

"Yes Brother. Thank you Brother."

***

As summer became autumn, the pain in my hips increased. Passing water became a dreadful task. I almost resented the existence of my cock, but the sexual adventures were still a very great pleasure that redeemed it. The dream of the long staircase recurred many times, but two other strange visions joined it. In the first, a young man, possibly myself, stood on board some strange giant ship of the sky that seemed to float above the Earth. It seemed a pleasant dream, but when I woke and walked into the garden, the sky disquieted me. In the second dream, I lay in a muddy hole on some battlefield. I seemed to be dead, part of the ground, and beside me lay a strange device. I wondered what it might be, but then I saw a man holding one similar. A crack of fire and thunder erupted from the black tip of the object. Death pervaded the dream thereafter, suffocating, like the stench of rotting ordure.

I also still dreamed of Him Downstairs. Satan appeared to me in my dreams and spoke of some wicked choice he would offer me. Each time I refused and each time I woke sweating. My death approaches, but somehow my idyll with Justyne seems the greater reality. Its joy pushed back the curtain of an uncertain death, so that I enter into it with a greater vigour.

I caught J crying again. However, now I could talk with an intimacy that one normally reserved for the closest friends.

"What is it this time?"

"Oh it's nothing. I don't like to speak of it."

"Well you ought to, now we know so much about each

other."

"I was crying, because I have learned of the suffering of one of our number."

"One of *your* flock?"

"In a way, yes."

"Don't speak in riddles. What do you mean? Who? What?"

"One of the sisters showed me a waste bucket full of red slop. She caught a lay brother with it and thought he might be smuggling wine. It wasn't wine but blood. She demanded to know its provenance. The Brother refused to tell her, so she came to me. I questioned the brother. He told me it was the blood of the most senior Brother working here. I believe you must know more about this than I… But I have seen blood in the piss before. It can be fatal. That is why I am crying."

"Oh. I see. But you, yourself, told me you were ill. Even if I am mortally wounded by this life, so are you. We should cry together."

"No. We should not cry. We must urge ourselves harder, push on, along the Pilgrim's road, as God is urging. I believe we *must*…" She could not find the word and added a distraught, "Oh!" before falling into my arms.

I comforted her, but one question niggled in my mind, one she had not answered clearly.

"Are you mortally sick?" I asked. She pressed her head into my armpit. I gently lifted her chin until I could look into her brown eyes.

"No Brother. Not like you." She smiled. Her smile seemed to me like the cracking open of an almond by the Sun. I laughed.

We had already finished the pulpit steps and reached the first landing of the flight of stone steps in the Chapel tower. The steps were cut to shape and finished, before carriage to the Monastery, at a local quarry of white limestone. This had proved the least expensive option, but one morning Brother Mattheu came to me, wringing his hands.

"Brother Arnaud, the Quarry Master sent me a note this morn. He has to put up the price for the steps!"

"*What*? But the price was agreed! It is a preposterous suggestion! Why?"

"He has had four deaths in the last winter and now has to support the families. He begs for your understanding, but the price for each step will now be increased to seventeen silver denier."

"We cannot afford that! Let me think. You are seeing him on your way home?"

"I wasn't going to, but I can if you wish."

"Good. I will have a reply for him by then."

I wrestled with the problem all day. A solution finally came to me, so I told Brother Mattheu:

"Ask the Quarry Master how much the steps will be *without* dressing."

"But Brother, that will leave us a lot of work and none of us are experienced…"

"Dressing is simple enough. I have seen it done. We will all simply have to work harder. I myself can organise the nuns to do most of the work. Ask him."

"Very well."

He returned in the morning with the answer.

"Without dressing, each step will be the same price as before. He said he is, 'Grateful for your indulgence.'"

"The obsequious serpent! I'm sure he *is* grateful! Very well, let us continue in this way. God frequently shows us that where there is a will in doing his work, there is a way. This is just His way of making us appreciate his work more greatly."

However, in truth, the work on the steps was grinding down our souls. It was a Sisyphean task, because the limestone wasn't the best and by the time we had finally dressed a step, the steps below it would be worn unevenly, so we would have to redress those. I myself took to making wooded shields, to be placed on the steps during our work.

***

The steps reminded me of those in my dreams.

At first I didn't think *ours* would be endless, but now I'm not so sure! We all spend a few hours a day grinding the limestone away and even when the lay-brothers had gone home Justyne and I continue for another while. My hands bled. The nerves became so numb that touching J's breasts no longer took me to the heights of religious joy and ecstasy. However, as the steps grew higher, I became filled with a Divine Passion, which I can hardly describe.

The culmination of weeks of anticipation came. We reached the second landing and I clasped Justyne's rough and bleeding hands in an ecstatic caress. When she prayed, so filled with joy did she become that she not only stripped to the waist, but kept stripping until she stood entirely naked. Her boldness almost struck me dumb, but a fever took me. My erectness became so long that it seemed to defy the probability of nature. Naked, we knelt together, skin touching, and prayed.

"We should continue work on the steps," she declared.

I nodded, so we continued to grind away the limestone with rough adzes. We must have looked like two ghosts, covered as we were in fine, white dust. It choked us, so I stood up to pause, gasped for breath and I saw how fat and enticing her bottom looked when she bent over her work. In our playground of redemptive work, we had pondered how to commit the final act of communion, but had not known how. No book I could find in the Scriptorium gave instruction. Sexual intercourse did not come within the range of practical matters within the bounds of Holy Teachings. Consequently, we were left to stumble, unguided through our Garden of Eden.

Approaching Justyne, I held my erection like the prow of an ancient ship, feeling felt like the mariner whose ends were unforeseen, but neither death nor life held any fear for me now.

"Oh!" was all Justyne uttered when my cock clumsily touched her white buttocks. She turned, saw the approaching member and, after exclaiming, helpfully spread her legs a little and continued to work. At first I could not find a way inside her warm, velvet purse, but then I felt something give and my cock slid all the way inside her. It felt a great relief to find that home that many men must have yearned for and I felt a rhythm growing inside me. I communicated this to her, reaching around to grasp her pendulous breasts firmly, to steer my ship through the treacherous mist. Together, we rode the rampant waves, but only when I groaned with effort, did she stop working and murmur something. It sounded like, "Blessed Holy Mother Mary…" but I could not be sure. The fluid of my religious joy overflowed me and coursed into her receptive body. We collapsed, spent, on the steps and some minutes passed before we took up our adzes and continued our work. We left the Chapel that night, content that we had done our best to achieve God's purpose.

***

The tower took on a slight lean, as we approached the third and final landing, the floor from which the bells would be rung. We were always a few courses below the completed walls, so had to crouch beneath linen sheets that sagged under the weight of water from the foulest weather. As the weight of the tower settled in the ground, it would occasionally sigh and list, first one way, and then the other. I feared for my very life, for the longevity of it, such as remained, on several nights of violent thunderstorms.

On just such a night last week, Justyne and I were discovered. We had many times achieved full intercourse since the first and believed we could hasten the tower's progress by our efforts. J often likened the tower to my erect cock "The beauty of this tower is somewhat like, but perhaps less than, your fully erect member," she commented. She found the word 'cock' too difficult to use. She admonished herself for this weakness many times and said a number of Hail Mary's in repentance.

I had just come out of her, and we were recommencing work, when we heard a loud cough. Suddenly terrified, for we knew an onlooker would not understand our endeavours, we peered in the direction from whence the utterance had come. I thought I saw a movement of the linen sheet, which sealed the Chapel from the Cloisters.

"Who's there?" I shouted.

No reply came, so I rushed to the partition. Pulling aside the cloth, I saw Brother Henri, making swiftly for the Chapel door.

"Brother Henri! Wait!" I shouted. He stopped in his tracks, but did not turn to face me.

"You are naked, Brother Arnaud!" he replied in a loud whisper. He sounded most distressed.

"Do not leave!" I implored him. "I will dress and we will talk. I do not know what you… think you have seen, but I wish to discuss it calmly with you. Then, if you wish, you may report it to the Abbot."

"Just let me go! I won't tell a soul. I do not want to be involved," he howled.

His anguish touched me, but I felt in no position to grant his wish. I commanded him once more and he turned. I dressed quickly and instructed Justyne to do the same. She was praying fervently, so I had to whisper her name several times before she complied. By this time, the stricken brother had returned to the linen partition and held it aside, to stare at us.

"Come in! Come in!" I implored. "Sit down."

"No. I cannot wait. My wife is expecting me. In fact, I'm very late. You see, I fell asleep! And then when I woke, I thought I heard voices, somebody in pain, behind the curtain. I felt it my duty to peer inside. I saw… well, I don't like to say what I saw."

Justyne's shoulders relaxed, so I felt less anxious after his explanation. I had feared he had resented my previous admonition and had been spying on us. If he had been, surely now he had enough evidence to see us go before an ecclesiastical tribunal, and even be burned upon a stake.

"Please… please let me go. I won't mention it to anybody," he continued. "Everyone knows monks are not always pure of heart and spirit. I have no wish to be involved in proceedings against you, to be involved in your downfall."

"But my admonition some time ago, on the matter of…?"

"*Now* I know why you asked. I didn't feel angry at the time and I'm certainly not now. We have looked to you for inspiration … But I'm only a simple man. I just want to eat my dinner and talk with my children."

I wondered if more words, or even a bribe, might be appropriate, so I glanced at Justyne. She simply nodded to tell me, "Let him go."

"Go then, Brother Henri. And thank you very much. We both thank you from the bottoms of our souls."

He smiled, turned and left.

***

The flames licked higher in the pile of wood under my roasting feet. Every breath I drew sucked in ash-hot air. Tears streamed from my eyes, only to boil off my cheeks. I glimpsed Justyne between the flames before she became completely wreathed in her own pall of smoke. She did not see me. Her eyes were almost of out their sockets as she stared into the heavens. Her lips moved ceaselessly, beseeching God and the Holy Mother for some kind of release from the suffering. But her eyes finally made me lose all hope of life. Their fear was mine, so I could no longer hide the truth from myself. I would burn, my flesh would melt and my life would end in one, long scream of agony. All my life, I had been afraid of fire and now the worst torture of Hell had been visited upon me.

The flames had almost reached to my feet, but for one stupid moment, I felt glad they were unshod, because they would melt more quickly and create a wick for the burning of my body. A moment later, however, I knew I wanted to live. Even a few more seconds would be precious. I smelled, rather than felt, the flesh on my feet melt. The heat seared my flesh so absolutely that it could have been ice water, but the smell, the knowledge of my own death, hurt beyond endurance.

"No, please God. Don't let this happen to me! Dear Father, whom art in Heaven, hallowed..."

The sound of screaming interrupted me. It sounded most like the deep rumble of a wolf's growl. The unearthly sound came from my left, so I knew it must be J.

How can a human make such a sound? They are truly Servants of Satan!

"You will all burn in Hell for this! Our *Father*, who *art*..." It took all my will to find the words in the depths of my tormented soul. The crackling of flesh drew much closer now. I guessed the hungry flames had reached my belly. Then I woke.

"You were having a bad dream Brother. I'm sorry for touching you but I had to wake you."

"I'm glad you did Brother Luc. It was a most perturbing dream! But I have overslept anyway. I must attend my duties in the Refectory." My time preparing food dragged like a ball and chain around my spirit's ankles.

After leaving the Refectory I went to the new Chapel, where Mattheu and his men were already hard at work. With every step, I expected the Abbot or a smug monk to call my name. Surely I would be confined and then sent for judgement. But nobody stopped me. Nothing seemed unusual, either that day or the next, or even the one after that. Indeed, apart from Justyne's understandable fraught state of mind, and the inevitable hiatus to our endeavours, life continued as if nothing had happened.

"Did anybody say anything to you?" she asked, in a rather rushed whisper when her first opportunity to speak with me came.

"No. Nothing. Perhaps Brother Henri meant what he said."

"All the same, we cannot do anything like that *ever* again."

I smiled, but I felt hurt. "No of course not!"

However, even though we appeared to be safe, something *would* soon change for me. Without the joy of our secret covenant, the rapture of our joint pilgrimage to the heights of the human soul, my body began to fail. The pain in my hips grew in its intensity over only a few days, until I could not stand. I had to be carried on a litter and could only watch the work on the steps, most of the time, from a rough bed. Whenever I felt able, I did some work to finish the stone steps. The brothers would lower me on the litter so that, face down, I could work with the adze between the handles of the litter. Other times I felt able to sit, albeit for short periods.

Pitying me, J came to sit with me in the evenings and we prayed where I lay, or sat. Her prayers were less fervent now, but mine more so. I felt my own death approaching too fast and I did not yet feel at peace. Monks are not supposed to write down our thoughts, unless we have the eminence of Saint Bernard, but I felt the need to record mine in a journal. If I was to leave this life before I had accomplished some inexplicable goal, at least I would record my efforts. I would hardly care which ecclesiastical tribunal would pore over my notes after I had gone. They could burn my bones then if they liked. I had jotted down some notes half-heartedly since we began work on the steps. At first I thought it might be a treatise on the sacrifice of man for a greater purpose, but now I want to write the truth, which is something quite different.

***

These are my last days on Earth. I am sure of it. Today I could barely lift a hand to do any of the work on the steps. With my bare fingers and J's help I managed to scrape a handful of loose limestone dust from the last step before the top landing. The pain in my bowels feels indescribable. I only hope I can live through this night and the next, so that I can see the steps completed. They have come to symbolise a journey for me, perhaps my journey to Heaven, but perhaps one to another, hotter destination. It's not my journey with J that makes me doubt my entrance to Heaven, but the vivid dreams I have every night now. Why *does* Satan visit me so often? Perhaps he senses I am near the end and he wants to get his bid in first. In any case he won't get me if I have anything to say in the matter.

What bothers me most is a thought I could not express until I talked with J and suddenly blurted it out. Now I will write in my journal that what bothers me is the thought that I am not me! What I mean is that I am somebody else. Perhaps you have seen that already, you who may one day read this. Perhaps you will have better knowledge of the world's workings. Perhaps you will understand better than I. Perhaps you will see that I have lived before. *Perhaps* you will see that death of my body means nothing. Perhaps… There are so many perhaps.

***

The steps were completed a few hours ago and I fear I will not survive to see the sun again. I have asked Justyne to make the last entry, hide my journal and sell it in the town when she reaches the end of her life. I don't want her to suffer, but I do want somebody to know what we saw, how *we* lived.

Brother Arnaud died just after the third bell this morning.
Sister Justyne

***

The Steps

It seems that even a holy man cannot resist the temptation of satan's choice.

But I haven't given up. I have had what seems like many lives to consider my encounter with Satan in the lighthouse and I think I see a chink in his armour. While despair could have overcome me, a dogged determination fertilised, somewhere deep in my soul. But at the moment I can still see no way out!

I have decided that I will tell you no more of those stories from the books in the library, my so-called 'lives.'

***

My mind, freed of any Earthly routine or focus, drifts frequently into long considerations on the nature of love. Such a one comes to me now:

I remember Chloe as clearly as in a dream. We were both jetsom of the wartime evacuation, buds in Somerset.

She stepped as lightly on the grass of the farm's fallow meadow as a faerie, but when we had crossed the minefield of pats to the stream, we splashed spritely in ice water.

A summer haze drew itself down around us, Avalon's last mist, ripe, refulgent with grassy cow-smells, soft loam and wind-whispered willows.

There, after a flash of silver leaped from a pool, I first planted my plain lips on hers and heard her squeal with pleasure.

Were it not for my mother's smacking hand being well out of reach of my soft, white buttocks, I would never have dared further. If the old man and woman who lodged us had not been childless, how could they not have known what universal chemistry would mix itself under the cover of our single bed, bestowing a supernatural boldness to my Archimedes fingers? They wormed, they spiralled until I felt her wetness, the round of her humped hips and the pink promise of her, as yet, unbudded nipples. She was a delight beyond all delights, until she parted her legs and I tried to explore inside her.

"No!" she yelped, and closed her legs against me like the gates of Heaven.

If only a boy of ten could understand, but I did not. Silent frustration turned to the first deep anger of my life, an anger that threw itself against the gates of her mind again and again until we were both too weary to speak. She asked for a separate bed, so I slept on the couch. I hated her then.

I wonder now if this hatred might have been the seed of a despair that grew in me, through my lives, always contaminating hope. This idea is all that stand between me and the total annihilation of my soul.

I guess it must have been in my life as Jason Andrews, or possibly Ariel Schechter, I'm not sure, but, anyway, some cousin seems to have been employed by the RAND Corporation and worked on Game Theory. I remember talking to him about it and, because it hadn't been taught on my Maths degree course, I had been hungry to know more. I have been applying the theory to my situation, so that I can understand what the Devil is doing, why he is doing it and whether I can win this game.

One has to make a few assumptions for my theory to work; first, that the potions or tablets always work and second, that the Devil is in control of his own game. The latter we should take with a pinch of salt because the theory, according to Christians, is that God is *always* in control. But locally, and in the short term, the Devil could control the game. The simplest game in game theory is the zero sum game; a game where both players stand to gain or lose exactly the same amount. This clearly is not the case here. I have my life to lose, possibly my soul, whereas the Devil is just doing this for pleasure. I would even venture that he would still get some pleasure, if I won and lived, because he could invent a new game, and a new life, in which to torture me again.

However, this is the interesting part; the Devil cannot possibly get so much pleasure if he *knows* he will always win. Therefore, I must assume it *is* possible to win. One of the tablets or potions must be innocuous. This gives me hope of course. Even if I am a modern-day Priapus, there may be a chance for me. But there are some worrying questions that arise:

Why is God letting his happen? Have I committed some great sin, that I should be tortured thus?

Also, what is the point of life, if one lives in permanent doubt? It seems that my doubt is what gives the Devil most pleasure. It is a most particular and dreadful pain.

And yet, perhaps, just perhaps, the Devil is testing me, doing God's work after all. How wrong it would be to condemn him when he may be doing good.

I have searched my memory to see whether I have ever lived without doubt and whether the doubt comes after the discovery that I am ill or before. I cannot seem to find the answer.

Damn these steps! I could think better if I had some light!

"If there is anybody in here, trapping me, you have to speak to me now … ! now … ! now … !"

"I don't think I can take this
anymore … more … more"

"Am I alive … ? alive … ? alive … ? Or dead … ?
dead … ? dead … ? dead … ? dead … ? dead … ?"

***

Opium

The last rays of sun reflected off the Pearl River, fingering the denizens' faces with a rippling, golden light. The wooden building sat low on stilts in a mosquito ridden pool of Guanzhou.

"Sometimes poverty is good," the old woman reflected. "But not often." Her next thoughts were glum, heralding the enuit which comes after a trip into paradise with opium.

"Girl!" she called softly.

A tall negress, dressed only in a single scarf of cheap red silk wound around her hips and breasts and sleek with moisture, nodded and left the room.

No doubt checking with my partner.

Like a well oiled machine-woman, the negress returned moments later, carrying a silver tray. She brought the large tray to the old woman and placed it on the rush-covered wooden platform, which ran around the large room. On the tray lay the accoutrements of an opium den's primary purpose.

For a moment, the old woman admired the younger negress' long, muscular limbs, which gave the servant that appearance of something sculpted by a greedy man. She felt a pang of envy, but dismissed it, immediately banishing any thought of making conversation. She never made friends with the den's 'maids.'

While the old lady lay back, the negress picked up the the bamboo pipe, which had been bound by circles of silver, depicting scenes of courtly love. She wiped the silver bit clean, to remove any saliva, and peered down the open end to check that the packing of palm slices and hair remained even and dry.

The negress laid down the pipe and removed the glass

lid from the opium jar, watching with satisfaction, as a single wisp of vapour curled away from the golden brown liquid. She picked up the needle-thin skewer and deftly dipped it in the liquid, while twisting it between her fingers. When she lifted the needle tip away, a single globule of the liquid, like a silver-brown pearl, clung to the tip and began to cool into a paste. Quickly, she placed the tip of the skewer in a small, glass bowl, filled with tobacco, and took a long match from a box.

By now, the old woman had turned to watch her, and gave permission for her to proceed. The negress handed the smoker the pipe, lit the match and gently heated the paste and tobacco in the bowl. The smoker breathed in deeply and sucked a stream of white vapour up the pipe and into her lungs. She took one more, long breath, before laying back, but before closing her eyes, she whispered:

"My head. Raise it. I like to watch the Pearl."

The negress didn't understand the last part, but dutifully raised the woman's head and plumped the pillow, before laying the woman's head upon it.

A golden light from the farthest sun swelled up and overcame the old woman. She felt the headlong rush toward eternal peace and infinite knowledge and, once again, her nipples and genitals tingled with the unspoken poems of a thousand heroic youths.

The negress watched the woman fall into that elysiacal trance and suddenly understood the request, having only recently learned the name of the River, which had borne the slave ship in from the ocean two years before.

***

For some reason she could not have explained, Adhiambo continued to watch the old woman's face until another customer called her away. She hardly noticed when the man beside the old woman stirred and pulled up the negress' silk to stare at her buttocks. The old woman wore a floral chèuhngsāam, the single-piece dress denoting status for a woman. Her face looked more riven by cracks than any other living face Adhiambo had seen. Clearly, this woman had survived many sins and yet she still seemed whole, carrying her bitterness only in her gaze.

Adhiambo felt glad when the woman recalled her to fill the pipe.

Sounds swirled into images of forgotten dreams, and the passions of many flower-boys ejaculated upon the throne of her mute desire, before the woman's junk sailed gracefully into port and her eyes flickered open. Now, only the night lights of passing freighters stole glory from a half-moon, skulking away behind the August clouds.

Such sights were the waking luxury of the old woman alone. As co-proprietor of the den, she had sole access to the prime pallet, opposite the single window, whose view eased the effect of leaving the opium-dreams. She sighed and raised her arm, which seemed easier than speaking, and the young negress came to her side.

"Another?" the negress asked, in pigeon Cantonese.

"No. I must soon get up. You are a good maid." The old woman surprised herself with this compliment, but continued, "Do the men harass you too much?"

"No. The opium makes them docile. I am lucky to work here."

For a long while the Cantonese woman thought about this, before replying, "No, you are not,"

"I want to marry, have children. I have money now. For a maid I do well."

"I'm not surprised. You're skilful with the paste… and have an elegant body."

The two women's eyes met and held for a few seconds.

"Thank you. You are wise and have led a long life."

"Ha! Rather, the other way round. Wisdom only comes after a lifetime and, sometimes, many lives."

"I need it now. I would marry. There *is* a man, but…"

"But?"

"I fear that if I have a boy, I will have nothing to teach him. My brother was a fool and died for nothing. I don't want that for my boy. What can I teach him?"

"Men never know what they want. They know what they *think* they want. It is for us to tell them, to show them."

"Yes, but this is for a man. What do I teach a *boy*?"

"Ha! You are not so stupid. I will tell you the story of the mouse. I had it told to me so very long ago and have almost forgotten it. Let me think… .

"Once, a farmer, no, a baker, had a problem with mice. His wife nagged him to kill them but he wouldn't. He loved mice, and all animals, you see?

"He tried every trick he could think of to make the mice leave his grain store, but they liked it there too much.

"There were two small mice, two parents and an old, wily mouse, who had seen many adventures.

"Eventually, the baker used poison and killed all the mice, or so he thought.

"One night, his wife had gone away to her cousin's, so he sat up, smoking. Imagine his surprize when he spotted a small bundle of fur on the floor.

"Looking closely, he saw it was an old mouse. He didn't know it at first but he soon saw that the mouse was too ill to move. It had eaten the last of the poison. 'On no. My sins are returning to haunt me,' he told himself. 'But I must accept this.'

"The baker kept still and, over the next few hours, the mouse crawled closer to him, rather than away. This confused the baker, because he expected the mouse to hate and fear him. 'I am so sorry,' he whispered to the mouse. 'I feel so bad. Come here and sit with me until dawn.'

The mouse eventually reached his feet and there it remained, waiting for its own death. For, you see, no creature likes to be alone.

"However, just before dawn the mouse felt his death approach and no longer wanted company. He crawled under a cupboard and quietly passed away."

"And what happened to the baker?"

"At dawn he took the mouse outside and buried him under a good hand of soil."

"Thank you."

"Teach your boy that no soul likes to be alone."

***

The End

Biography of Lazlo Ferran

During Lazlo Ferran's extraordinary life, he has been an aeronautical engineering student, dispatch rider, graphic designer, full-time busker, guitarist and singer (recording two albums, one of Arabic music featuring the rhythms of Hossam Ramzy). He has traveled widely and had a long and successful career within the science industry but now left employment in the public sector to concentrate on writing. He has lived and worked in London since 1985 and grew up in the home counties of England.

Brought up as a Buddhist, in recent years he has moved towards an informal Christian belief and has had close contact with Islam and Hinduism. He has a deep and lasting interest in theology and philosophy. His ideas and observations form the core of his novels. Here, evil, good, luck and faith battle for control of the souls who inhabit his worlds.

He has traveled widely, living for a while in Cairo during 1982. Later, he spent some time in Central Asia having various adventures, one of which was getting married in the traditional Kyrgyz style. He has a keen interest in the Far East, Middle East, Asia and Eastern Europe - the latter informing his series of books about vampires and werewolves. He keeps very busy writing in his spare time and pursuing his other interests of history, genealogy and history of the movies.

From the author:

Thank you for reading my story and I hope you liked it. I value very much feedback from people and need this if each book is to be better than the last, so if you could take the time to post a comment on my blog or simply email me, I would appreciate it.

Where to find Lazlo Ferran
Blog: http://www.lazloferran.com
Email: lazloferran@gmail.com